Praise for Harriet Scott Chessman and *Lydia Cassatt Reading the Morning Paper*

"Written in the precise, yet elliptical style of Virginia Woolf."
—*The New York Times*

"Chessman, like Lydia herself, has allowed herself to inhabit another's world with grace and humility."
—*San Francisco Chronicle*

"Harriet Scott Chessman's story . . . adds to our understanding of these paintings and to our understanding of the painter's life. One feels the author's magnifying glass over their lives, with its genteel distortions and the enormous eye of the writer."
—*Los Angeles Times Book Review*

"Chessman burnishes the simple moments of ordinary life with an elegant meditation on art and flesh."
—*The Women's Review of Books*

"One of the most talked about books of the season."
—*Book* magazine

"How delicately, how perfectly Chessman considers the subtle currents of love and jealousy that mingle in this sibling relationship . . . In Chessman's compelling story, [Cassatt's] paintings seem more alive than ever."
—*The Christian Science Monitor*

"A moving story of courage and creativity . . . Chessman, with pitch-perfect prose, has penned a celebration of family, love, and art."
—*Arizona Daily Star*

Harriet Scott Chessman is the author of the acclaimed novels *Lydia Cassatt Reading the Morning Paper* and *Ohio Angels,* as well as *The Public Is Invited to Dance,* a book about Gertrude Stein. Formerly associate professor of English at Yale University, she has also taught literature and writing at Bread Loaf School of English and at Wesleyan University, and has published several essays on modern literature. She lives in the San Francisco Bay Area with her family.

ALSO BY HARRIET SCOTT CHESSMAN

Lydia Cassatt Reading the Morning Paper

SOMEONE NOT REALLY HER MOTHER

HARRIET SCOTT CHESSMAN

A PLUME BOOK

PLUME
Published by Penguin Group
Penguin Group (USA) Inc., 375 Hudson Street, New York, New York 10014, USA
Penguin Group (Canada), 90 Eglinton Avenue East, Suite 700, Toronto, Ontario, Canada
M4P 2Y3 (a division of Pearson Penguin Canada Inc.)
Penguin Books Ltd., 80 Strand, London WC2R 0RL, England
Penguin Ireland, 25 St. Stephen's Green, Dublin 2,
Ireland (a division of Penguin Books Ltd.)
Penguin Group (Australia), 250 Camberwell Road, Camberwell, Victoria 3124,
Australia (a division of Pearson Australia Group Pty. Ltd.)
Penguin Books India Pvt. Ltd., 11 Community Centre, Panchsheel Park,
New Delhi – 110 017, India
Penguin Group (NZ), cnr Airborne and Rosedale Roads, Albany,
Auckland 1310, New Zealand (a division of Pearson New Zealand Ltd.)
Penguin Books (South Africa) (Pty.) Ltd., 24 Sturdee Avenue,
Rosebank, Johannesburg 2196, South Africa

Penguin Books Ltd., Registered Offices: 80 Strand, London WC2R 0RL, England

Published by Plume, a member of Penguin Group (USA) Inc. Previously published in a Dutton
edition.

First Plume Printing, September 2005
10 9 8 7 6 5 4 3 2 1

Ⓟ REGISTERED TRADEMARK—MARCA REGISTRADA

The Library of Congress has catalogued the Dutton edition as follows:

Chessman, Harriet Scott.
    Someone not really her mother / Harriet Scott Chessman.
        p. cm.
    ISBN 0-525-94793-0 (hc.)
    ISBN 0-452-28697-2 (pbk.)
    1. Holocaust, Jewish (1939–1945)—Fiction.   2. Parent and adult child—Fiction.
3. Reminiscing in old age—Fiction.   4. Mothers and daughters—Fiction.   5. Dementia—
Patients—Fiction.   6. Jewish families—Fiction.   7. Jewish women—Fiction.
8. Grandmothers—Fiction.   9. Connecticut—Fiction.   10. Aged women—Fiction.
11. France—Fiction.   I. Title.
PS3553.H4225S67   2004
813'.54—dc22   2004007176

Printed in the United States of America
Original hardcover design by Leonard Telesca

PUBLISHER'S NOTE
This is a work of fiction. Names, characters, places, and incidents either are the product of the
author's imagination or are used fictitiously, and any resemblance to actual persons, living or
dead, business establishments, events, or locales is entirely coincidental.

How then, she had asked herself, did one know one thing or another thing about people, sealed as they were? Only like a bee, drawn by some sweetness or sharpness in the air intangible to touch or taste, one haunted the dome-shaped hive, ranged the wastes of the air over the countries of the world alone, and then haunted the hives with their murmurs and their stirrings; the hives, which were people.

—Virginia Woolf, *To the Lighthouse*

Hermione.   Tell me, mine own,
Where hast thou been preserved? Where lived? How found
Thy father's court?

—William Shakespeare,
The Winter's Tale, V, iii, 123–125

To Libby Wolf,
with gratitude and love

ONCE,
SOMETHING

*M*orning here is not like any mornings Hannah Pearl has ever known. First, the young woman with hair the color of honey comes in. Her hair spills out of the barrette. She's wearing a blue—uniform.

"Upsy-daisy, Hannah!" she says, raising Hannah's bed. "Here's your glasses!" She opens them up and puts them on Hannah's nose. "And here's your medicine."

On the young woman's uniform is a small—something— with *Roxie* on it. Of course she is Roxie. Hannah swallows her pills, one at a time, with water.

On this morning, the young woman—how is she called?— adds, "You're having a visitor today, Hannah." She smiles as she flips Hannah's quilt off, and her sheets. "Time for the bathroom."

One arm behind Hannah's back, one holding Hannah's right hand, the young woman pulls her upright. Slowly, Hannah sits on the edge of the bed. The young woman bends to pull on Hannah's slippers, her honeyed hair almost touching Hannah's knees.

"All set, Hannah. Now here's your walker."

"Merci, mademoiselle."

"I love it when you call me that! *Mademoiselle.* I've got to get my boyfriend to call me that, it's so elegant." She holds Hannah's elbow gently.

Hannah holds on to the silver handles and walks slowly to the bathroom. The young woman helps Hannah sit on the toilet. While she waits for Hannah, she looks into the mirror quickly, and tucks a strand of hair around her ear.

"Sharon will come give you your shower in a few minutes. So don't you want to know who your visitor will be, Hannah?"

The young woman says *Hannah* like *hand,* with an *h* bold and blowing, just like that, and an *a* flat, like a marsh. Hannah is used to this, but privately she thinks of her name as having an *h* only when you write it. When you say *Hannah,* the word should open up at first, with no *h* at all, just a lovely "Ah!" and then another one. "Ahnah!" with more fullness to the second "ah." How to tell the young woman this?

"Hannah? Don't you want to know who's coming?"

Hannah thinks of a rhyme. *Who's to visit Mrs. Pearl, Mrs. Pearl? A doctor, a something, a something, an earl.* She is worried about splashing the floor, so she concentrates on making a single stream as the young woman—how is she called?—stands close by now, touching her shoulder. Hannah also likes the other one, with the warm voice, who sings. Her voice makes Hannah think of something her mother used to make—something warm and sweet, with pears. That one billows the new sheets like wings, like parachutes, as she sings.

"Hannah? Did you hear me?" The young woman is squatting down in front of Hannah now, smiling. "Your daughter's coming this morning! She comes every week, right? She isn't from France, like you, though, is she?"

The young woman's words puzzle Hannah. She had a daughter, true, although that was in her other life, and how could her daughter, so young, find her here? This place—who could know where it is? The halls go on and on, making a puzzle. One can become lost just going to the—big room for meals. Hannah wonders how to say this.

"This—" she begins.

"Looks like you're done. OK?"

The young woman takes a few sheets of toilet paper and wipes Hannah briskly.

"I can do that myself," Hannah says.

"Oh, I know you can, Hannah, but I can just do it so much quicker. Up we go. Wash hands."

Breakfast comes after a wait in the dining room. "English muffins," says the woman who serves her. The other women are chatting together, but Hannah isn't listening until they say, "Hannah, how did you sleep last night?" Hannah cannot remember how she slept, so she nods and says, "Very well, thank you."

The woman with bright red hair says, "You'll come out with us this morning, won't you, Hannah? We'll ask for permission to take you. It's a gorgeous day for a little walk, a perfect spring day. We could walk just up the block, to see the marsh through the trees." Oh, Hannah knows this woman, of course she does!

"I think her daughter, Mir, is coming this morning, Helen," says the woman with white hair and dark brown eyes. She's drinking her coffee, black. She is small herself, and a little hunched over. When she looks at Hannah she winks.

Hannah spreads butter on her muffin as she eyes the eggs all folded in on each other, with smooth walls. She could cook eggs more deliciously than this. A bright picture comes to Hannah of a kitchen, soapsuds frothing, her own hands warm and clean. Something's about to go into the pan—eggs with a bit of milk, a bit of cheese—and something's baking in the oven—Hannah closes her eyes to see and smell—little rolls for lunch.

Words come floating, out of a yeasty ocean: *and, all in tears she melted, dissolving, queen no longer, of those waters.* Who wrote this? Hannah loved Ovid in translation, and Shakespeare. A delicious language, English.

"Did you say something, Hannah?" the one with red hair asks, touching Hannah's hand with her own. She's a friend, Hannah's sure now; both of the women are friends.

"She melted."

"Ah. She melted, eh? Sounds like not such a good thing to do, no? Melting is not so good."

Hannah smiles.

Soon she's sitting in her chair by her bed. Outside the window the leaves wave, light green, new ones. Here in her room

is her rug, braided with many colors, and her bed, and her—
wooden something—with round circles one pulls, and her
mirror, and of course her closet. Inside her closet, she is certain, wait important—documents. One day, possibly, she will
look at them. She hopes for their safety. If the young woman
with the honeyed hair comes in, Hannah will ask her to
check. Maybe she will ask her to hide them.

Hannah's hands look like landscapes, moonscapes, with
ridges and valleys, changing with movement. She likes looking at them against the color of her skirt, a color like the little round fruits, bloodred, purplish, one picks from the tree
in the garden. A something—a pit!—inside. Someone
younger picks them with her, and drops the basket. Fruits
scatter over the grass.

How has she come to have a skirt of this color? Maybe the
young woman has given it to her. *Un cadeau.* Inside this language another waits. Hannah catches glimpses of it, like
looking into the windows of a train going slowly past, as you
stand in the field nearby. Hannah rubs her eyes. She does not
like to think of trains.

When a woman comes in, Hannah is startled. She's tall,
wearing high heels, and she walks briskly, as if she's on
her way somewhere important. Her hair is shiny and her
eyes look quick and lively. She has the air of someone
from outside.

The woman comes close to Hannah and squats down,
holding her hands and looking her straight in the eye. Pretty
eyes, like shells. A mermaid, maybe. Hannah knows she's

being silly, but she glances at the woman's feet for a hint of fin or scale. Mermaids drown you. They sing, though, too, don't they? Songs like air.

The woman's asking Hannah questions—so many! How to keep track? She asks one and, before Hannah can begin to understand it, she moves on to another. She talks quickly and her words rush together.

Now the woman is quiet. She squeezes Hannah's hands— ouch!—and says something Hannah can grasp.

"Out." That's what she's saying. "Let's go out for lunch." *Sortons, sortons!* Hannah pictures *Maman*, shooing plump Auguste, tail bristling, out of the kitchen. Out where? Hannah wonders. Not to a garden. Wall leads to wall. Someone will stop them. A line becomes a circle. You always come— home, she used to say.

The woman is looking at her with a question in her eyes. Hannah feels uncomfortable. What is she supposed to say? She doesn't want to venture out, near the place where the women sit and talk on the telephone, in blue uniforms, in white coats.

But, "Out," she says, in spite of herself, and nods. The woman looks happy now, as if she has plunged into clean, icy water on a hot day. I plunged like that once, thinks Hannah, proud for an instant, in another country, the pebbles hard on my feet, someone calling to me, *Viens, Hannah! Vite!* Come quickly!

"Yes, out!" says the woman. "To a restaurant! Where would you like to go?"

Where, indeed? Hannah pictures a house, cream colored,

one of many all attached, glass with lovely colors in it—blue, red—in the window of the front door.

"I—" she begins, but the woman is too quick.

"Shall we go to the Pomegranate? You always like that restaurant. It's the French one, remember? Remember the veal? You like it with the mushrooms, remember? Or what about the Golden Wings?"

What is she talking about? Hannah's glasses start to slip down her nose; she catches them and fixes them. How is the woman coming up with names like this, Pomegranate, Wings? She must be mistaken.

Not wishing to hurt the woman's feelings, Hannah smiles, and the woman smiles too. She is American, Hannah's sure. Hannah notices how her eyes look puzzled—sad, maybe. She has a little line just above one of her eyebrows—how is that called? A something line.

"How about if we just get in the car and decide once we're driving around?" The puzzled look changes into a hopeful one, and suddenly Hannah senses how her own kindliness toward this woman is blossoming into something else, courage perhaps. She decides to go along with the woman's hopefulness about a restaurant outside. She can't remember the last time she felt so ready to try for a change. To change places, why, that is a change indeed.

To Hannah's amazement, the ones at the desk do not say, "Wait a minute! Where are you off to, Hannah?" as she and the woman walk up the hallway. A couple of them just keep looking into the big pink drawers filled with papers, or putting pills into little cups. One of them, in a white coat, looks up.

9

"Taking Queen Hannah out for lunch?" she asks.

Hannah wonders why the woman calls her this. Hannah looks at her shoes carefully as she walks, slowly, slowly, with her silver walker on its quiet wheels, the pretty woman's arm around her.

"Yes! We're off! I just have to sign her out." The woman picks up a pen and writes something on a—white thing.

"Don't get her back too late! She needs her beauty rest, you know!"

The pretty woman holds Hannah around the waist.

"She's beautiful enough," she says.

"*Au revoir!*" says the woman in the white coat, only it doesn't sound right.

"*Au revoir, madame!*" says the pretty woman, laughing, with an accent just so. Perhaps she is not American after all.

Now Hannah walks down a hallway she cannot remember, past door after door. Outside one door, an old lady is stuck in a wheelchair. She looks twisted into an inhuman shape, like a squash or a cucumber that grew all wrong. She stares at Hannah with yellowed eyes, and Hannah almost trips, because the stare makes her forget what she's doing. That staring one looks as if she would like to hold on to my ankles, thinks Hannah, and she wonders how to tell the woman about this possibility, when, miraculously, they reach two big doors, and the woman pushes one of them open.

Sunlight. Hannah blinks. The light warms her face and arms. Outside is a season. No soldiers, unless they are hiding, spying on her, behind trees.

"See how the leaves are coming out?" the woman asks.

Hannah looks at the leaves, pale green and small. So many trees, arching like—women moving, bending. She sees yellow flowers under a tree with white—skin.

"See how the daffodils are up now? Remember our garden in New Haven, on Livingston Street? Remember the daffodils you planted out front, by the walk?"

Hannah rummages inside herself for a garden with yellow flowers. She pictures instead a small garden with a stone wall and a flowering tree. She has a sense of something vanished where something was (*and, all in tears, she melted*—who wrote that?). She pauses to look at the woman, who's rushing on to name other parts of this splendid picture, all in light, laid out in front of Hannah now. Blue sky, she talks about, and forsythia, a boy on a bicycle racing along, the smell of the marsh, and—"Look! Here's my car!"

Hannah looks. *"Tiens!"* she says. The car is white. How full of courage Hannah is. *I am placing myself in this car, under this woman's wing, and who knows where she will take me?*

As the car moves, Hannah looks out the open window. She sees houses, and gardens, and children holding their mothers' or grandmothers' hands. Soon a green park spreads out in a square, with shops and churches around it in rows. A woman walks a dog; a child is held high on shoulders by a young man in a sweater the color of—sky.

Hannah pictures a square, not green but stone, in the city she once loved, a little table at the café near the cathedral, orangeade, a child tossing crumbs to the pigeons. The child's eyes like almonds.

"The library," the woman says, slowing the car a bit as she passes. "We could get some books for you after lunch."

Hannah sees a walkway leading to a big—place—brick, with glass.

"Remember when I would sit on the elephant, in the library in New Haven, the one at the entrance to the children's section?"

Hannah laughs—a delightful idea, she thinks, a woman on an elephant! Delightful too, to think of a place with an elephant inside. What a grand day this is indeed!

And lo and behold, the woman is right. Here am I, "out," thinks Hannah, and in a restaurant with the name of Pomegranate. How many people have not been able to come to such a place? Her family—elsewhere—would delight in the white cloth covering the table, the pink flowers, the sky-colored plates. She enjoys the menu—*Menu,* it says, right at the top, with names of luscious-sounding things below: poached salmon with dill, lamb with rosemary, pear salad with goat cheese. It's lovely to have all the names in front of you like that, in light golden lettering. Hannah touches her glasses and bends forward.

The woman suggests the lobster bisque as an appetizer, and then the salmon. Hannah nods happily. A delicious lunch is just what she would like.

"You can share a bit of my wine, too, although we'd better be careful, because of your medications."

Once the bisque comes, Hannah listens to the woman's story about someone named Conor, who might be her husband, and of her job at a museum, "curating," she says—a word Hannah contemplates.

"I'm a curator, Mom, right?" the woman says, looking as if Hannah surely must know this already. "Of American art, *you* know."

"Of course," Hannah says, although she doesn't know. She wonders what a curator does, and she begins to have a worrisome feeling that she's supposed to know this too.

Then the woman talks about her children. Hannah's sure they're her children by the way she says their names, so casually: Ida and Fiona. She's having a pleasant time listening to a story about how the woman took her children to the beach one summer, many summers ago. Hannah's bisque is lovely, and soon her spoon clinks on the bottom of the bowl. The bowl disappears and a plate of salmon arrives.

"Could we have more bread, please?" the woman asks the waitress.

"Oh, of course." The waitress whisks away the basket.

"Remember? I looked around, and she was gone."

Hannah stares at the woman. She wishes to ask who was gone, but she feels shy. She begins to think she knows these children, Ida, Fiona. Perhaps she even knows this beach.

"The waves are small," she says, "not like an ocean."

The woman smiles quickly. "Yes, small. It's on the Sound, Mom, remember? Fiona lives in that town now, right, with her baby? It's the town next to this one. The beach is sandy, and you like to look at the rocks, just offshore. Remember we picnicked there just last summer? The water isn't too wavy, and sometimes you can walk out on the sandbar. But at high tide it gets deep quickly."

Hannah tries to picture such a place—she almost has it!—yet another shore sails in front of her, pebbled and sandy, both, her own legs small as the rough water crashes and then rushes over her ankles. *"Viens, mon cœur!"*

The waitress brings a mound of bread in a basket. Hannah is sure now she should know much more than she does.

"I couldn't believe it. She'd been right there, digging a big hole with Fiona, both of them with their long legs and their hats on backward, and bringing buckets of water to fill the hole with, and all of a sudden I realized I hadn't seen her in ages. Remember, we asked Fiona where Ida was, but she had no idea."

Hannah enjoys her salmon. How did she used to poach it herself? A dry white wine, garlic, and herbs—which ones? She listens to the story in a distant sort of way, until the woman touches her arm, and Hannah looks at her.

"Do you know where I found her?"

Hannah shakes her head. Suddenly the question of where children disappear to puzzles her enormously. Maybe the world has holes in it, she thinks, but she knows this can't be so.

"In the water, swimming way out. Way too far out. I called to her, and she waved as if nothing on earth was wrong."

Hannah pictures a girl swimming far out at sea, and she begins to notice she's trembling. A terrible urge comes upon her, to look for something—someone. So that's what has

happened. All this time, she has neglected something—someone. She must not continue in this way.

"I—" she begins. "I have to—"

"Go to the restroom? I can help you."

Hannah waves her away and shakes her head. *"Mais, où
est ma—"*

The woman bends close to her and touches her arm again.
Her hand is strong and warm.

"Where is your—your what—?"

Has she changed, grown younger somehow? wonders
Hannah, puzzled, because right before her eyes this woman
is someone new, someone Hannah knows, knew—someone
young, in a house Hannah knows, knew, all right, the American house, yellow, in a city, on a shady street, lush in summer, wide steps leading up to a porch. And inside, this girl's
hair alight—the color of honey!—on the pillow, or wrapped
around her fingers as she sits at the kitchen table, writing
something for school, and on the stove is something for
breakfast—French toast, as they say in America, and on the
counter are Hannah's poetry books, her students' essays and
poems to be read late at night, after her daughter has gone to
bed, her daughter—and her daughter's name comes to her
now like a dove, plump in her hand—Miranda.

"Miranda," she says out loud, and the pretty woman
looks startled, as if she's seen a ghost.

"You know my name," says Mir. It sounds like a question
and a fact, both.

"Miranda. Mir," Hannah says again, and she squeezes
Mir's bare arm. *How did you become so old?* Hannah wishes

to ask. *Where did you go?* The restaurant, the pink roses, the plates, all seem to hold still, become simply a picture, as Hannah touches Mir's arm. *And Ceres, secure and happy in her daughter's presence*—Hannah read that somewhere—how full of beauty words are! The world cannot always match such beauty.

Rushing into Hannah now, a huge wave of images—of *knowledge:* her yellow house on Livingston Street in New Haven, Connecticut, with Mir in it, and an apartment before that in the other American city, with a "brook" in it, and the subway Hannah took to school, to work, her baby with her cousin Julianne and others, and another place before that, in another country, the city with Russell in it—London!—and another, of course, *of course*, in the place of her family. *Rouen.* Looking into Mir's blue eyes, surprised and yearning, Hannah sees the cheekbones, the mouth, of Russell Pearl, not French, but English.

Hannah caresses Mir's cheek, the lobe of her ear, pierced by a small silver circle, with a drop of—light—swinging from it. She rests her hand under Mir's chin, and smiles at her.

"You really know me," Mir says.

Hannah nods. "*Oui. Je te reconnais.*"

"You can talk to me in English?"

Hannah thinks. "Yes," she says, carefully, wondering, suddenly, if she says it right, without an accent. People always listen for an accent. Her mother had one; she brought it with her from Russia. The woman at the—how do you call it? *la pâtisserie*—made an ugly face when she heard *Maman's* voice. She wouldn't serve her, although she was next in line.

16

Yet the same woman smiled at Hannah's father. Of course she smiled; he was handsome, a real Frenchman. *Maman* had come to France when she was already seventeen. *Papa* was a—*un Juif, comme Maman, mais*—to go to the synagogue! Oh, he was always too tired. Sometimes they quarreled about it. He was a doctor. He loved her mother, though, in spite of her accent, in spite of her first home being Russia; of that, Hannah is sure.

Miranda is holding her hand as her hand holds Miranda's chin.

"I have missed you so much," Mir is saying. She moves closer, looking as if she has something important to ask.

Gazing at Mir's face, Hannah knows something more, *how Russell folds her into him, on a bed in his little flat in London, on his night pass, the windows blacked out, German bombers flying overhead, the hissing sound of a shell heading toward its blind mark, so close, and then the* boom, *huge, shaking the room, the bed, Russell and Hannah, his face invisible in the English dark, but his words, breathed along her cheek, It's all right, Hannah, it's missed us.*

"That one missed us," she says to Mir now, nodding reassurance.

Mir looks puzzled. "I missed *you*," she urges.

"You were safe, Mir. Not born."

Water fills Mir's eyes. She holds Hannah's hands with both her own, hard.

"What are you talking about, Mom?" she asks, using the funny American word.

Hannah remembers (*oui!*) *Maman et Papa, Tante Louise,*

her sister *Emma,* all vanished (*comment? pourquoi?*), leaving Hannah to live on (*how? why?*), in the English country first, and how could she have kept living if she hadn't had the baby, born squirming and innocent? Innocent of history, this baby (Mir!), with her blue eyes; she came soon to smile, and to search for nourishment and safety in Hannah, all of twenty-one years old.

Hannah shakes her head. She's lost the thread. Why is Mir crying? Her daughter.

"It's all right," Hannah says. "You're safe here." She looks out the window, to see small trees shaking with small leaves. Hannah scoffs at her own worry. Of course there are no soldiers, no bombs speeding toward this restaurant from the sky. She bends her head to look up through the leaves. Not even an airplane. This is a new country, as she has always known it to be. Even in the fields, the parks, no land mines to blow you apart, to bloody the limbs of someone you love.

To move to a new country (*Oh my America!*), Hannah thinks now, looking away from Mir's sad face to her own hands, old, wrinkled, with brown splotches on them, like stains. To move to a new country is to slip past a veil, hiding there from here, then from now—a necessary fiction, but always a fiction, because then is always now, here is always there, and in the midst of this fiction began her struggle to become something solid in this most solid of places. *I'm studying to be a teacher,* she would say, her efforts, at dawn, at midnight, to write something else—something more—down on paper (*I'm a poet,* she wished to say). Her daughter growing up somehow, leaving home, marrying the handsome young Irish Catholic—Conor McCarthy!—(chicken served in a cream sauce, ham and cheese, whisky, a Christmas tree and painted Easter eggs—Hannah shudders, yet he loves Mir, after all), having her two girls, living in a small Connecticut town near the inland city, an hour away—all of it seems to roll up into a strange, rich poem.

"Mom, can I tell you about Ida and Fiona now?"

Hannah nods.

"Well, Fiona you know about, because she comes to see you, right? She's pregnant with her first baby; it's due in October." This information sounds urgent, the way Mir says it.

Hannah nods, although she is uncertain about a baby. Fiona is a beautiful child with blond hair. She sings Hannah a song; how does it go? *Oh, sandwiches are beautiful, sandwiches are fine, I like sandwiches, I eat them all the time.*

Hannah bends toward Mir. "She likes to sing," she says.

"Sing? Yes, I guess she does like to sing."

I eat them for my breakfast and I eat them for my lunch, if I had a hundred sandwiches—

"And Ida—well, Ida." Mir seems to search for the right words. "Ida's going to graduate from college, in May. She'll be in France this coming year, remember?"

France? Hannah feels worried. She knows two Frances. One is before, one is after. *Once, later, she found the house with Mir, and a dog barked at them. A woman refused to let them come inside. The house was hers, she said. Hannah wished only to look inside, and she almost asked about her Auguste, until she remembered how old he would be. Cats do not live as long as people. Yet perhaps she could just see the cherry tree for a moment? The woman shook her head and shut the door firmly.*

"She must be careful," Hannah says.

Mir laughs. "Oh, she'll be careful enough."

How can Hannah tell Mir about the dangers? She wishes to protect her, she has always protected her, and now look what has happened. Mir has sent her own daughter to the place where so many vanished, children too. Hannah cannot think of all that.

Mir touches Hannah's hands.

"She'll be fine, Mom. She's twenty-two years old."

At twenty-two one is a mother. Hannah looks out the window and sees a car drive slowly up and then back slowly into a—place. She sees a man inside. He looks at his—the round thing on his arm, above his hand. What country is he from. She shivers.

"Cold?" Mir asks, smiling. "Shall I help you put your sweater on?"

Hannah shakes her head. What can a sweater do? Mir doesn't see what Hannah sees. Always, it has been this way. Perhaps Hannah is at fault for telling her daughter so little. Is one safer if one is ignorant? She hopes, in any case, that Mir doesn't notice the man, who slowly pulls himself out of his car, looking up the street and down the street.

The customs officer looks at her passport and her visas, slowly, slowly, in the midst of the noise and the chaos, people rushing, bumping into each other, with suitcases, pulling children by the hand. It is May, and the Germans are said to be rumbling with their tanks toward France, something one could not even dream of. Hannah has rushed here with Papa by train, to the port at Le Havre, but Papa has to go back to Rouen; she has said good-bye to him, hurriedly, her throat hurting, as she must have said good-bye to Maman, yet she can't remember, she can't remember how Maman looked, or what she said; she can't remember her face! And she can't remember saying good-bye to Auguste or to Emma either— could she have forgotten something so important?—and now the officer looks slowly at her documents as if no one else is in line, only to look up and stare at Hannah. Vous avez de la famille en Angleterre? *he asks, and Hannah prepares herself to lie, for Papa has told her to say she has family in England, although they are only friends of friends really, he has told her to show the letter, and also the letter from the English family, who have given her the position of au pair. Papa has promised to come with Maman and Emma as soon as possible, and Auguste too, if Rouen becomes uninhabitable. Yet before she says a word, the officer lights a cigarette, and stamps her passport, and she is free to go; she walks slowly, jostled, up the ramp to the ferry, holding her heavy bags, Papa nowhere in sight.*

The waitress hands Mir a piece of paper.

It is perhaps better not to promise.

"Ah!" Mir says. She moves her hands away from Hannah's. "Wait just a moment, Mom. I have to do the bill. After lunch we can have a nice walk on the green together, OK? I have so much to tell you. I haven't even told you yet about Conor's new commission, for the restoration of a gorgeous old building in downtown Hartford, and . . ."

21

Mir looks up from the piece of paper. Hannah tries to picture this Conor.

Hannah smiles. She knows Mir is asking for a smile. She looks out the window again, but the man has disappeared. Maybe he is in the restaurant. Hannah knows she must hold her eyes to the table. She studies the remnants of her dessert on the white tablecloth—a fragment of chocolate cake and slivers of—something, shaped like Emma's eyes.

Au secours, she wishes to say to Mir. But, as she looks at her daughter, adding up numbers on a napkin, Mir changes, or, Mir has been whisked away, like Hannah's dessert plate, like Russell in a meadow, like Hannah's family, and in her place sits a middle-aged woman, frowning at a piece of paper and writing something. Hannah feels herself slipping out of this present, this lit-up place where—she's sure—she held knowledge, like a bird, in the palms of her hands. As she looks at the lovely woman, she pictures herself opening her hands and saying, "Go!"

DOVE

*I*da McCarthy looks at the folded sheet of paper: *125 Hale Street, fifth house on right.* Her professor, Mr. Shipman, wrote these words in blue pen in the upper right-hand corner. The rest of the sheet holds a draft of the first half of her newest poem, which is pretty good so far, but frustrating, just like the others. You can get a good start, but something happens in the middle; it spills over its boundaries, becomes diffuse, like a marsh. How to go on with it?

She's written eight poems so far this spring for her college poetry seminar, all of them about her Grandma Hannah, from one angle or another. This one is a sestina, a form she's only tried a couple of times before. Ida loves how the words she's chosen for the end of each line in the first stanza—*face, glass, rose, cut, glimpse,* and *more*—hold new positions in the next five. It's a slow and surprising circling, an intricate dance. If all of life could hold such beauty! This poem—she might call it "Face to Face"—is in Grandma Hannah's voice,

25

as Ida imagines it, writing to a *you*, the young Englishman Hannah married, with the odd and romantic name: Russell Pearl. Grandma Hannah's whole story is romantic, in a way, but it's incredibly sad too, how she escaped France in 1940 when she was fifteen, only to lose her family at Drancy and Auschwitz; how she married Russell Pearl in England, only to lose him too before Ida's mom was even born. Ida still doesn't know how he died.

You can't think about such a life too much, or you'll feel too helpless, too despairing, not only about your own family, but about people in general, what terrible things they do to each other. Clinging to Ida, though, like a hoary old barnacle, is a persistent and crazy yearning to rescue Grandma Hannah's family, or else to change their story; can you just scrape such a feeling off? Fiona seems to—she lives very much in the present, with the adoring Hodge, their picture book cottage, and now her pregnancy to round out her happy and unhaunted life.

Ida adjusts her backpack. It feels so heavy today, in this warm spring sun. As a child Ida used to dream about helping her grandma escape. Sometimes in the dreams Hannah would be Ida's age, and Ida would find her in a hole in the ground, or under a bed, and Ida would pull her along after her as she raced through a field, down a city street. Sometimes Ida became a bird-girl, as Hannah rode on her back, clinging to her neck, and in rare dreams Ida would discover a godlike capacity to reach down from the sky with one feathered hand as she flew with Hannah, to grasp the arms of Hannah's family and whisk them out of a clutching and bony crowd. Each flying dream held the frightening possibility that Ida herself would be pulled down to earth, and into the hands of soldiers; often Ida would wake up sobbing as she fell out of the sky, Hannah and the others falling with her, just as Icarus plummeted in the painting Ida used to gaze at with Grandma Hannah on the sofa, the big book of art on her grandma's lap. *Can you find Icarus?* Grandma Hannah would ask, and Ida would point to the tiny figure, unnoticed by anyone else in the picture—the ploughman, the sailors— yet noticed triumphantly by Ida. *Très bien!* her grandma would say. *But why doesn't anyone see him falling into the water?* Ida would ask. *People don't always notice such things,* her grandma would say briskly, turning the page. *Ah! Look at this one!*

Not that Grandma Hannah has ever appeared to be in need of rescue. She's always been independent, happy on her own, at least until a couple of years ago, when she had to leave her house in New Haven, filled with art and books, the fragrance of her kitchen, to enter Tikkun, a nice place near the water, with pretty views, but isolated. Ida can't imagine living anywhere with just old people, no matter what you can look at out your window; her grandma liked to talk to people of all ages. For the first year there, she was as busy as usual, always hopping onto a shuttle bus to go to a museum, to the symphony, to neighboring towns for shopping. Her friends came to see her, as they still do, the ones who are still alive, and she made new ones too, Helen and Rose and the others, although a couple of months ago she had to be moved to the assisted living wing, where she could have more supervision. She'd started to just take off, with or without her walker, down the street, who knows where she was going, and when someone would try to help her, she wouldn't be able to tell them anything: where she lived, her name, her phone number, her closest living relative.

A mail truck pulls up to the curb and a mailman steps out. He nods at Ida as he crosses the sidewalk in front of her to head up to a brick house, where a little biscuit-colored terrier goes crazy yipping and clawing at the window. Hale Street must be close. Has she missed it? Ida looks at her watch: twelve-fifty, and her appointment with Mr. Shipman is at one o'clock. A woman is puttering about in the garden in front of an old cape, a bucket for weeds and clippings on the lawn beside her. A boxwood hedge makes a border. Ida looks at the blue sky through the tender-leaved trees as she walks. It's so pretty here.

Only once does Ida remember Grandma Hannah crying— no, twice. The first time happened when Ida was about seven or so, at Grandma Hannah's house on Livingston Street in New Haven, before she sold it. Grandma Hannah was babysitting her and Fiona, and Ida had been playing outside in the dusk with Fi, trying to catch the one or two fireflies that came over the hedge into Grandma's yard. As the dusky sky grew deep blue and then charcoal, Grandma Hannah called them in, and of course Fi went right away, but the summer night was soft and magical, and before Ida knew it, Grandma Hannah's voice had risen to an alarming pitch—*Ida! Viens ici! Viens tout de suite!*—and Ida, slipping into the deeper darkness under the pine tree, began to worry that her grandma would slap the backs of her legs, as she'd done once, so Ida stayed quiet, barely breathing, the pine needles pricking her bare feet. Fiona was practicing the piano by then, some intricate piece, and the notes wrapped around Ida with searching grace as a car's lights glimmered through the hedge. It was only when Grandma Hannah started to make embarrassing, gulping sobs that Ida, chastened and disturbed, came slowly up the porch steps.

The second time, Ida must have been a little older. Standing at the threshold of Grandma Hannah's kitchen, she saw her mom and Grandma Hannah at the table, Hannah's shoulders shaking, her hands over her face. Ida's mom, catching sight of Ida, waved her hand and frowned as if to say, *Shoo! It's all right!* But how could it have been all right? For Ida her grandma's crying struck her with the intensity of an illumination. She felt certain, as she stood in the threshold, as certain as if God had sent a dove into the kitchen window with a letter in its beak, that Grandma Hannah was crying because she missed the people she never spoke of, the ones in the photographs she kept in the deep bottom drawer of the bureau in her bedroom, the ones whose fragile letters she had tied in packets with yellow ribbon.

The bottom drawer smelled sweet and musty; Ida always thought of this as the smell of history, too precious and too terrible to know. And yet she wished to know, she couldn't help it, her questions popping out of her mouth whenever she had a chance and before she could think. *Can't you be quiet for once?* Fiona would say. *Can't you see Grandma doesn't want to talk about that?* Only a handful of times could she lure Fi to open the drawer with her when they visited

Grandma Hannah in New Haven. It was on one of those furtive occasions, in the white lace cleanliness of the bedroom, that Ida discovered Grandma Hannah's poems, written out in black pen on special paper. Once she searched further into the drawer's layers, to discover a batch of sketchier poems in pencil, words crossed out and new ones substituted. *Listen to this one, Fi,* and Fiona would sit impatiently, looking over her shoulder every few seconds to see if the door was opening. *What's so great about a bunch of poems?* she would say, but Ida thought they were magnificent. Why had Hannah hidden them away like this? Ida told Fi she would make a book out of them, if they were hers. Fiona preferred to gaze at the most romantic photos, especially one of a thin young officer with curly light hair, holding a cigarette in one hand as he embraced a girl, his face bent to hers in a luscious and full-mouthed kiss.

Ida comes with relief to a sign for Hale and turns right. So this is Mr. Shipman's street. She becomes aware, as she walks past the first house, how much this neighborhood reminds her of her childhood home in Wethersfield, just an hour away, inland. Forsythia bursts in yellow bloom. A bucket of chalk lies spilled on a lawn, the chalk drawings half rubbed out on the walk. A springer spaniel watches her from a front porch, reminding Ida of her old collie, Lily, who'd wait on the porch and then rush to greet her as she'd jump off the bus. Ida feels homesick for a moment—surprising, how homesickness swings into this bright spring day, for she's been fine at college for almost four years.

Walking toward Mr. Shipman's house, she has again the dreamlike sensation, dizzying and odd, she's tried to push away since this morning, thinking about his suggestion, when she bumped into him outside the English Department building, that they meet at his house this time. His children get out of school early today, he said, and he has to make sure to be home. He seemed rushed and a little distracted, as he wrote the directions on her poem, and Ida found herself blushing and saying fine. Of course she was stupid to blush; it's normal to have a conference at his house, especially if he has children. Other professors must do this sometimes. Why should Ida think it's so extraordinary? Yet she hasn't told a soul.

The third house on the right is yellow, a gingerbread house with lattice under the eaves. A small tree in front still shimmers with silvery eggs for Easter. Looking at her clogs as she walks, more slowly now, Ida tries to think about her poem. She hopes Mr. Shipman likes it so far. He likes her decision to pull all her poems together into one sequence; she might call the whole collection *Dove*.

"Why *Dove*?" Mr. Shipman asked, in her first conference with him. He bent toward her in his office, his elbows on his knees, all his books in bright colors on the shelves behind him: Yeats, Bishop, Stevens, Neruda, dozens and dozens of poets. On his walls, abstract art, yellows, reds, in gorgeous lines, and bits of paper Scotch-taped to the wall near his computer. Outside his windows lay snow, and on his desk, a framed photograph of rocks off a shore, the sky clear blue. "I don't know, I just like the sound of it—a dove bringing an olive branch after the flood, to show Noah there's hope, there's dry land somewhere. Like for my grandmother, she had to find some kind of hope in the midst of such sadness—at least, I think she must have." "Ah," Mr. Shipman said, and something about the way he said "Ah," the stubble on his cheek, the way his pale yellow linen shirt was unironed and had the sleeves rolled up, the way he bent toward Ida, his hazel eyes (or were they gray?) sharp and interested, as if she filled the room somehow, made it lighter. Something about all this had touched Ida and made her shake, almost, with more happiness than she had ever felt with someone before. Her hands started to shake, in fact, something that embarrassed her, and as she stood up to go, she knocked over the paper cup of coffee that had been sitting on his desk—cold coffee, luckily, as Ida discovered; it spilled all over her jeans. "Oh, I'm sorry," she said, and he offered her a napkin, saying, "Not to worry! I'm sorry my cup was so near the edge of my desk." She hastily dabbed her jeans, grabbed her heavy backpack, and walked quickly out of the room. She glanced over her shoulder just as she reached the door to see her teacher standing by his desk, a kind smile on his face. "I'll see you soon," he said, and Ida, flustered, nodded and fled.

Ida comes to the fifth house. It's large and pretty, a white Victorian with a wraparound porch and green shutters. She has been imagining something more like a contemporary, all glass, with Japanese plantings, just angles and light, like in one of her dad's architecture magazines—a house in which to write the kind of poems Isaac Shipman writes, philosophical and abstract, contemplative, beautiful. This house is in some disrepair, a couple of steps needing to be replaced, the outside in need of a new coat of paint. Her dad would never let a house go this long between coats, but then he loves getting up on a ladder; it's relaxing, he says, although her mom tells him to be careful, she has enough on her hands without caring for him in a wheelchair. As a kid in West Roxbury, he worked for a painting company each summer—something he loves to tell Ida and Fiona, whenever he's about to paint a bathroom, or the kitchen, for the fifth time—and he misses the smell of fresh wood and paint. When he does the whole house, first he power-washes it, and then he takes at least a week, after work and on weekends, repairing boards. Yet her dad would fall asleep over a book of poetry; he falls asleep in front of the TV, these days, the new collie, O'Hearn, asleep on the couch beside him with his long nose comfortably in her dad's lap. The house is so quiet now, as if it's waiting for something to happen, for someone to return.

Ida runs her fingers through her red hair, moves its thickness off her shoulders. She should have put it up. *Ida, look at you!* her mom used to say in despair when she was little, if she'd come in from playing all day in the meadow and woods near the house with neighborhood kids. For school, her mom had pulled her tangle into a French braid. As she goes up the pebbled walkway to the front steps, Ida wonders how she looks now: Pretty, or ordinary? Sexy, or just nice? How old, how young? Not too young, she hopes. How old is Mr. Shipman? Twenty-eight, at least—he has kids! Ida glances at her new jeans, the ones she just bought with the money she saved from her spring-break job at Westfarms Mall. She's wearing a new tank top under her black sweater. Holding tight to her poem, she wills herself to think about the fourth stanza, the one giving her all the trouble. The first line has to end with *glimpse*.

On the wide front porch, a marmalade cat, mounded perfectly on the railing, eyes Ida warily and then feigns sleep. A few flats of flowers and herbs lie near a child's baseball bat and a big red plastic ball. Ida has barely rung the doorbell when Mr. Shipman appears, looking distracted but welcoming, his hair a bit uncombed, as if she's surprised him.

"Hello, Ida!" he says, opening the door wide. His shirt is lemon yellow, his hair uncombed. "Thanks for coming." He looks outside. "Did you walk all this way?"

"Oh, it's fine. I like to walk, I walk all over the place." Ida steps into the hallway. "Actually, I have a car, but it's at my sister's right now, because she needed to borrow it. She lives just down the coast, and her husband's traveling, so I . . ." Ida is aware that Mr. Shipman has a quizzical look. "Well, anyway, it's fine."

"Good. Well." Mr. Shipman smiles, looking uncertain for a moment, as if he can't remember why Ida is here. Could he be shy? Ida wonders, the thought a new one, not fitting. The hallway is large, opening out at the back into a kitchen, and to the left into a big living room, the oak floors just a little scuffed and littered with a small sock, a tiny green soldier, children's drawings, crayons, and a pink mouse catnip toy with yellow spots. Ida imagines children running through the hallway, chasing each other as she and Fiona did. *Fi! Wait up! Can I play, too?* She broke her arm, once, running after Fiona, when Fi slammed the door behind her as Ida flew into it. It had almost been worth it, to see how sorry Fiona had felt later.

"Should we—sit down?" Ida asks.

"Yes! Of course!"

Mr. Shipman opens a door to the right, and Ida follows him into a room looking out onto the front porch. The floor is oak here too, but more polished, and white shelves hold hundreds of books. A light oval desk, made of maple, maybe, seems to float in front of the bay window, with a red swivel chair.

"Oh! Let me get you a chair!" Mr. Shipman goes out of the study and comes back in a moment with a plain wooden chair, straight backed. "Here. Have a seat."

And, if this is a dream, how gorgeous it is, to be sitting in Mr. Shipman's study, in his house on Hale Street, on a Tuesday afternoon, showing him her poem and listening to his thoughts about it, careful and kind (*this phrase is lovely, just right; I don't know about this word; you're straining here),* watching his hand as he holds your paper on top of an art book (Picasso, it looks like), and makes small squiggles in pencil. What would it be like to be married to such a man, who knows so much and is so good-looking? To wake up each morning to those hazel eyes (or are they gray?). What would it be like to be touched by those hands? Ida wonders for a moment if her own mom and dad, who barely seem to notice each other sometimes, had such happiness at the beginning, even an iota of what she has right now, sitting seven feet away from this brilliant man, reading her poem. Fiona, of course, has been happy with Hodge for five years; pregnant now, she shines, as if her happiness can't be contained. Always Fiona has known how to have what she wants. Ida's the one who knows what disappointment's like. *My disappointed child!* Ida's mom used to say, when Ida was little, stroking her hair, smiling ruefully. *You must be happier with what you have!* But Fiona's hair was straight and fine; she got A's even in math; she had dozens of friends. Ida felt disappointment in advance. She knew she could never catch up.

Ida realizes with a start that Mr. Shipman is quiet now, just looking at her. A hot flush rises from her neck up into her cheeks as she raises her eyebrows and smiles hesitantly. She hasn't been listening. Mr. Shipman rubs his chin and looks at the sheet of paper again.

"So, anyway, I think you should just keep going with it, follow it out."

Ida nods. "I'll try. It's just—it's hard."

"What's hard?"

"Well, to know where to go with it, I guess." Ida feels like an idiot.

"You clearly have an understanding of the form, though; you know what you're doing." Mr. Shipman hands the paper back to her. "How do you see the second half?"

"I'm not sure. I'm trying to figure out, for one thing, how Hannah feels about this Russell—how she feels about marrying him, and getting pregnant, and then having him die before her baby comes. I don't even know how he actually died."

Mr. Shipman looks thoughtful. "Well, do you have to know?"

"I'd like to."

"You could make it up, couldn't you? Hannah's your grandmother, but she's also a figure in your poem."

"I know, but I want the poem to be truthful."

Mr. Shipman smiles as if Ida has said something funny. "If you write your poem well, it *will* be truthful."

"Yes, but I mean *really* true."

"But how would you know what her inner world is, anyway? You aren't your grandmother, certainly not when she met her—this man, Russell."

"That's just it. I'm not Hannah, and I know so little about her, and now she's losing her memory, so I'll never know more." Ida is surprised at how this spills out. "Actually, she never talked about all this. She talked about all kinds of other things, but not this, not the War. It's like this big silence at the heart of her life—actually, in my own life too, growing up, because my mom never talked about it either. Only sometimes, a little bit would come out, and I'd be—well, stunned, but then that would be it. You'd have to hold on to these little bits, and try to piece them together on your own."

Running through Ida's mind was the sequence of questions she would ask her mom, and the short answers her mom would make before turning to something else: *How did Grandma's husband die? I'm not sure. Did Grandma ever talk about it? Not really. Did he die in the War? Just after the*

War, I think. What happened? Was he sick? I just don't know, Grandma Hannah never said. You mean you haven't ever asked her about your own father's death? I try not to ask her anything that would upset her. Why does it matter so much to you, Ida? He died! End of story! But it does matter. How could she say it doesn't?

The room is quiet. A dog barks somewhere. A woman's voice calls to a child. Far away a car honks.

Mr. Shipman looks at her gently. "It's funny about families, isn't it, how little you can know, sometimes, about someone you might love very much."

So you know this too, thinks Ida, her eyes quickly filling. She senses herself opening quickly, layer by layer, like a rose, like a wave, to this person, this Isaac Shipman, bending toward her in this room. She wishes to give him all she can, to say, *Here, hold this for me:* Grandma Hannah's house with the secret drawer; the sound of sobbing on the front porch; Fiona's pregnancy; Grandma Hannah's confusion; her mom's worry and exhaustion; the questions hovering always in the air, ignored and insistent, like ghosts; Ida's yearning for closeness. Because isn't love simply this—closeness, knowing what's inside another? *In the light of the porch, her grandmother's hands over her face. When Ida comes onto the porch, Grandma Hannah holds her fiercely. I thought I had lost you.*

"I always wonder," Ida says to Mr. Shipman, "how can you know someone better? I mean, someone you love?"

"I don't know. Maybe you write about them."

Something in Mr. Shipman's look, something tender and unspoken, crumbles a seawall inside Ida. How do people find love, anyway? She wipes her eyes with the back of her hand, and how it happens then she doesn't know, but Mr. Shipman is not seven feet away, but close, his hands in her hair ("Ida," he's saying, "Ida"), and she's crying and almost laughing too, her arms encircling him, her lips finding his, so real and salty, the stubble harsh on her skin, so that she feels herself swimming somehow in rough waves, caught up, buffeted, her mouth open, the sea rushing in, and before she can think, his hands are pushing up her sweater, her T-shirt, and she loves the feeling of him on her breasts, her nipples, but it's then that she pushes him away, pushes his mouth away, pushes his hands away, pushes away Isaac Shipman, an Isaac now, someone real and not a dream.

"God, I'm sorry," he says, sitting back on his heels beside her, covering his eyes with his hand, and Ida hesitates, yet she can't help bending to him now, because his contrition is even more appealing than his eagerness for her, and she kisses him again, searching for more salt, more swell. She slips to the floor onto his lap, her legs around him, and she's caught up in the kiss now, her hands on his shoulders, his neck, the smell of his skin something lemony, something briny, and she's sailing now, in the heat of it and the arching and the rushing, and all she can think is, *This is mine, this Isaac is mine. My own secret, no one else's.*

How many minutes or hours later, at the threshold of the kitchen, Ida lingers, watching Isaac Shipman, his yellow shirt unbuttoned, his feet bare, rummaging in the fridge.

"Could I give you some juice, Ida?"

"Sure."

"Apple or orange?"

Ida hesitates. She feels oddly like a child, just home from school.

"Oh, water would be fine. I should go in a second."

"Sparkling water, or just tap?"

Coming into the kitchen, looking over Isaac Shipman's shoulder, Ida sees jugs of milk, cartons of Tropicana, a half-full jar of apple juice, a bowl of leftover chicken legs, fizzy water, children's yogurts in bright containers. She wishes to touch Isaac's back, to feel the skin under his shirt, the warmth of him, but instead she walks to the sink at the kitchen window. A slippery avocado pit sits in a glass jar, its bottom half in water, toothpicks propping it up. Outside, the marmalade cat sleeps on a chair near a large rectangular garden bed, its soil recently turned and ready for seeds. A tricycle waits on the driveway, a swing under a big tree.

"I have to go," Ida says hurriedly. "Don't worry about the water."

Isaac turns to look at her, the fridge door still open.

"Ida."

How she walks out of the kitchen, how she opens the front door, how she can't help turning to kiss Isaac full on the mouth, his scent still salt and lemon, and something more now too, how she turns again to walk across the porch and down the stairs, how she looks over her shoulder to see Isaac in the open door, his face illuminated, worried, yearning, tired, utterly known and not known, loved and spurned, regretted and kept safely somewhere inside her, she has no idea. As she finds her way down the pebbled walk, her vision blurry, she holds the poem tightly in her hand. She's crying now, but as if on the horizon, or around the next block, she senses the first line of her fourth stanza waiting patiently for her arrival.

THY ETERNAL
SUMMER

*S*uch a morning already! Hannah is on a splendid and exhausting outing: marshes, she's glimpsed, houses, and stores with signs—CHILDREN'S CLOTHING, THE HARBOR BOOKSTORE, TRAVEL! In the distance, a thin line of something beautiful. "The Sound," says the woman in the car. She's wearing jeans and a coat the color of bread. Her hair is reddish, with a line of silver at the top.

"See the Sound, Mom? See how blue it looks today?"

Hannah worries; does she know this woman? The woman touches her arm; she says "Look!" She starts up the car, she slows down, she waits at the light. She talks quickly, her words swirling like leaves. "Remember this? Remember that?" But it is not so simple to remember.

The car goes now along a small street, sand at the edges. Children chase each other; one of them is crying. A dog the color of—toast—is walking with a boy whose hair is ruffled by wind. A woman is pulling long stalks from her garden as—milky things—sail above trees burning yellow and—other colors.

"This is Fiona's neighborhood, remember, Mom? Her house is coming up in just a second. And Ida should be here, too, by now. She's come all the way from Paris to see the baby. We're having a little birthday party, for the baby and me—remember, my birthday is in a couple of days?"

The baby? *At twenty she is a mother.* Big white birds hover over the small—tops of houses—crying *Aaah! Aaah!* One of them parachutes down to a sandy patch at the edge of the street, just ahead of the car, and doesn't budge. The car slows.

"These seagulls are either stupid or brave," says the woman. "Here's Fiona's house, in any case."

The car pulls to the side of the street. The white bird looks straight at Hannah.

The woman bends her head near Hannah to look at a house the color of—milk—with two windows and a door in front. Pink flowers spread out, straggly, near the door. The lawn is covered with yellow leaves, like a feather bed. Yellow leaves wave on a tree.

"Look! There's Fi, and she's holding the baby!"

Hannah looks. Inside the window, a young woman is holding something in her arms. She has a cloth over her shoulder.

At twenty. Your husband, is he in the waiting room? No, no. The English nurses are brisk. They can't be bothered to smile, to wipe Hannah's forehead. You'll be all right; babies are born every day.

46

The door opens, and out comes a girl, her hair a cloud the color of—fire—around her shoulders. She tiptoes across the yellow leaves with bare feet.

"Hello, Grandma!" The girl opens the car door and pops her head in, kissing Hannah on both cheeks.

"Ida! Where are your shoes?" says the woman. She walks around the car to embrace the girl.

"Happy birthday, Mom."

"Thank you! Did Hodge pick you up at the airport?"

The girl looks at the yellow tree. "Actually, a friend picked me up."

The girl runs her fingers through her thick hair. She brings her face close to Hannah's.

"Can I help you out of the car, Grandma?"

Hannah is on a soft couch, and all the women are busy around her. The woman with the silver in her hair comes in and out of the room. She brings Hannah a cup of strong coffee with hot milk, just the way Hannah likes it. She brings a glass of milk for the young woman nursing her baby on the couch near Hannah. She brings a glass of water for the girl, with a bit of lemon in it. She brings something warm with apples, and cuts it into slices, one on each plate. All of them talk quickly, only the young mother is sometimes more quiet, looking at her baby nursing, his tiny hand in hers, his gulps and snuffles noisy and lovely.

Four women lie crying out in pain and fear, Hannah one of them. Your baby will come, whether you complain about

*it or not, says the nurse. Outside this room, could there still
be a world?*

"I just wish I could get some sleep. I'm so exhausted. Yesterday he wouldn't take a nap at all, all day long. It was impossible. And I just stood in the garden, walking up and down, sobbing. How do people do this?"

"You'll be all right, Fi," the older woman says. "The first week is the hardest."

The girl slips onto the couch on the other side of the one nursing, and touches the baby's feathery hair with her finger.

"What does it feel like to nurse him?"

The young woman laughs. "Well, I think you can imagine what it feels like, Ida!"

"Really? That good?"

Hannah tastes her—something delicious. Someone has made it well, with a hint of—almond, is it? Something more, too. Cognac.

"Do you like the apple tart, Mom?"

"*Oui. Merci, madame.*"

"Mom, I'm Mir. You don't have to call me *madame*. I'm your daughter!"

*In the hospital, Hannah cannot help crying, she cries
for hours in the room with one window, high up. If she
could just die. A bomb hurtling right through the window
could not be worse than this. Inside, Hannah is on fire; all
is lost, all.*

"I am never doing it that way again!" says the young woman. "You can't believe the pain!"

"Don't tell me about it!" cries the girl.

"No one tells you these things, though, Ida! It's terrible, how no one tells you; it's like a huge conspiracy! Next time I'll definitely have an epidural."

"Isn't that a shot in your back? I hate shots!"

"I do, too, but it has to be better than trying to do it without anything. What was I thinking?" The young woman looks at the older woman standing by the window folding clothes. "And I know, I know, you told me so! You did tell me I should have an epidural; I just couldn't believe it, and by the time I asked for one, they said it was too late."

"I'm sorry, Fi. I hate to think of you in pain."

The girl jumps up, tossing her hair over her shoulder. She quickly puts the plates on top of each other, one, two, three. Two forks clatter to the floor.

"Damn!" she says, and bends to pick them up. She goes out of the room.

"Come back, Ida! I promise I'll stop talking about it! I'll only tell you the happy stuff!"

"I just need a breath of air," the girl calls. "I'm just stepping outside for a minute."

The walls are gray, like dirty water. Time to get this baby out, says the doctor; how would that be, Mrs. Pearl? He gives Hannah a shot and she can remember nothing, nothing. And then it must be over, for Hannah wakes to another room, big and full of beds, women resting; outside the windows, gray daylight. So Hannah is still here, after all. A woman in the bed next to hers has a flower in a vase, she asks, is it your first, then? Yes. A little girl? Yes. She's

*lovely. Hannah holds the small one in her arms, and it is
the only warm being in the world, the only one Hannah
can hold. Is your husband coming along today, then? No.
No, he's not. Hannah looks at the floor, bare tile. It smells
of antiseptic.*

The young woman talks softly now to the older one.

"At least Hodge was there, but he could do so little. He
kept saying 'Breathe!' and I shouted at him, '*You* breathe!'"

She laughs, and the baby starts to cry. She raises him to
her shoulder and pats his back.

"It's OK, Seamus! It's not your fault!"

*If only Russell could be here! Look! Hannah would say,
and Russell would kiss her, he would kiss the baby tenderly
and hold it close. We're safe now, Hannah.*

The young woman is singing a song about a little goat, in
the language Hannah's mother sometimes spoke. *Unter Seamus viegele, Shteit a klor vaise tzigele.* How astonishing that
she knows this song! *Seamus lernen Terah.* Something about
her—her voice, her mouth, her brow—disturbs Hannah, like
the eyes of someone in an old photograph. A little white
goat.

Yet, before Hannah can think how to say this, the singing
stops, and the women rush on, talking about first this, then
that, so quickly that Hannah cannot follow: where the young
woman's dad is, how he has to work today, because of a
building in Hartford, he's been ridiculously busy for months,
and it's too bad he couldn't be here, but at least he saw the
baby on the first day, in the hospital, and what's the matter
with Ida, she's been acting so weird since she arrived from

France. And how soon will Hodge get home, and Fiona needs to lie down for awhile, for she must sleep as soon as the baby sleeps.

Now a girl is in the doorway of the kitchen, her hair (the color of amber!) spilling, her arms crossed, her face bright and troubled.

"Are you all right, Ida?" asks the woman with the silver.

"Of course I'm all right!"

"You look . . . well . . ."

"I'm fine!" The girl walks away again. The room is quiet. A shadow crosses the floor in swift flight.

"I think I'll just lie down for a few minutes," says the young woman with the baby on her shoulder. "I wish Ida would stop being so dramatic. She always makes me feel I've done something wrong."

"Don't worry about Ida."

"That's like saying, 'Don't notice that hurricane!' "

"Go lie down, Fi. I'll hold Seamus."

The young woman (is she Fi?) wraps up her baby in a yellow blanket with little ducks on it. She gently hands the baby to the woman and shuffles, slowly, out of the room. Her hair is dull and messy; her sweater has a hole in it. Hannah could mend it if she had a needle. She could brush her hair. *She brushes her granddaughters' hair—how are they called?— "Don't pull, Grandma!" they cry, and she tries to be gentle, yet she brushes quickly, just as Maman does. Her own hair is braided in two minutes or less, and quickly she's off to school, her head aching.*

The woman holds the baby and sways, sways, her cheek

touching the baby's head. She walks out of the room. A little white goat.

Hannah opens her eyes. A girl—a young woman, really—is sitting right next to her, with her feet tucked up underneath her. Her face is close to Hannah's.

"Grandma, did you know I'm going to visit London when I go back?"

"*Ah bon?*"

"I want to see where you lived during the War."

How easily the girl says this. Hannah cannot look at her.

"Do you remember the address? It was in Regents Park, right? Where you were an au pair for that family—what was their name?"

"Oh," Hannah says. So many names! Sometimes they spill, and no one can stop them. Why does the girl want them?

"The Cliffords," says a woman with silver in her hair, coming into the room. She folds a blanket; she tidies up; always her hands are moving. "I have the address at home, Ida; I can find it for you."

"Grandma Hannah took care of their children, right?"

"Yes, Leah and Catherine Clifford. Mom has letters from them. She wrote to them at least once a year for a long time."

The memory comes, in spite of Hannah's wishes. It comes, and pulls her into *the hallway smelling of dampness and coal, lamb, boiled potatoes. The English children love her; their mother is always out. They have servants. Hannah is the au pair. The youngest one is small for her age, with blond hair.*

She follows Hannah up the stairs, down the stairs. She is not Hannah's sister, though. Hannah's sister is in grave danger.

"What was it like with the Cliffords?" asks the girl.

"Oh, I—"

How can Hannah describe this? *How she aches for her home, with the cherry tree in the garden, Auguste on her lap as she studies. How she aches for peacetime, for her old life in France. She cannot sleep in the cold room at the top of the English house, pigeons cooing stupidly outside, sirens in the distance, booms, and in the dawn, the all clear. It is difficult to hear this other language all around her. The English people do not ask about her family. Only the children ask. Each day the papers tell of terrible things across the Channel; how can she know what is happening? She waits for letters, and when the letters get through, she is happy for a minute only.*

"I don't think Grandma wants to talk about this. Could you help me in the kitchen, Ida? I want to clean out Fiona's fridge, and make something for their dinner later." The woman touches Hannah's knee; she bends to look into Hannah's face.

"Will you be all right, Mom? You can just rest a bit here, OK?"

Hannah smiles. She knows the woman is asking for a smile, and this is simple enough to give. What is it they have been talking about?

The girl sighs. She pushes herself off the couch. She follows the woman into the kitchen. Hannah listens to the way their voices lilt as the water runs and glass clinks.

What has Hannah been remembering? Something about a

damp kitchen, smelling of lamb, of mint, of coal. Something about walking in rain, her cold hands holding an umbrella, and—yes!—the warmth, the brightness, of a tea room, fragrant, consoling. Is this a dream, or is this real? Perhaps Hannah is dreaming now, for a young Englishman sits at the table next to hers. She cannot understand all the words on the menu. *May I help you? he asks, his face lit up, eager. His hair is light and falls on his forehead. His eyes are blue. Thank you, she says. Soon she is walking with him. He gestures excitedly when he talks; he touches her arm. Once she meets him in the park, on a bench, and he draws her close; she trembles in their kisses. Often he buys her lunch in a restaurant: little sandwiches, thin slices of cucumber and watercress, cheese and ham—delicious! He buys her English pastries. Hannah has so little money to spend. It's all right, I have plenty for both of us! he says.*

And one day she comes to his flat. It is winter, and she comes to him at the window, and lets him discover her curves, her hollows. Hannah, he says, pulling her closer, rushing. I do not want a baby, she says. I know, I'll be careful. It is painful, at first, yet Hannah feels safe on this bed, like an island, this boy's arms around her. And are you my family now? she asks. Yes, he says.

And one day she says good-bye to the cold room at the top of the house, the English people who do not ask about her family, even the little girls who love her, and she comes to stay. She cannot let Maman and Papa know, ever.

She can only say she teaches French and works at a department store, selling baby clothes.

A musical sound startles Hannah—Mozart, maybe, a cheerful sound, tinkling. Has she been sleeping? A girl with hair the color of—dawn—comes rushing into the room in her bare feet.

"That's my phone, Grandma!"

She opens her bag and pulls out a little silver object.

"Hello?"

The girl looks quickly at Hannah. She turns away. She looks out the window as she holds the tiny silver phone to her ear. Yellow leaves fly in the air. She says something Hannah can't hear, and then she says quietly, "Yes, I'll think about it."

The girl puts the phone away. She stands by the window, gazing at the floor. Hannah wishes she could stroke her hair, just as she stroked a child's hair once in porch light when the child came out of the shadow of a pine tree. *I thought I had lost you.* Little goat.

"Et alors?"

The girl shrugs.

Something comes to Hannah now, not a memory, but knowledge, right here in this room. She knows what this is, to stand by the window, to gaze at the floor.

"You are in love," she says.

The girl raises her eyebrows; color comes into her face.

"What makes you think that?"

"Oh." Hannah waves her hand in the air. How to explain? "It is not always a happy thing, to be in love. Sometimes it is happy."

"You were in love, weren't you?"

"I love a young man in the Royal Air Force."

"You mean Russell Pearl?"

"You know him?" Hannah feels a rush of gladness. Into this room, Russell has come, she feels, eyes alight, eager, full of hope. *Stay, Hannah. Come to the bed with me, will you? I will. It is painful at first, and Hannah knows it is not right, yet all the world is crazy now, and Hannah is so alone. This bed makes an island, safe from the world. Hannah, he says, Hannah.*

"I couldn't know him, Grandma. He died before I was born."

Hannah is doubtful. If he died, could he be here right now, so real, just out of sight, yet somehow in this room? Look! Is he not in this sunlight coming in through the window? Is he not in that bird swinging past?

Listen to this poem, Hannah, do you know this one? His chest is bare. He's making toast in the milky morning light. Shall I compare thee to a summer's day?

"How does it go? *Shall I compare thee?*"

"Oh, I know some of that. It's a sonnet." The girl stands by the window. Her face brightens. "*Shall I compare thee to a summer's day? Thou art more something and more temperate. Rough winds do something the something buds of May . . .*"

"Rough winds do shake."

"Shake, yes!"

After supper, cheese and eggs sometimes, sometimes sausage, Hannah kisses him and pulls him to the bed. She cannot wait to have him now; she cannot wait. Later, the booms begin. All of London is black and waiting. Hannah keeps the blinds down, yet she knows buildings are burning, only a mile away or less. At one in the morning, Russell pulls the sheet over them and turns on a torch. He kisses her and opens a book. At least we can die reading! But Hannah does not wish to die.

"Did Russell Pearl like poetry?"

"Oh!" How can Hannah describe this Russell? "He has a—a book—to write words in."

"He wrote poems?"

"*Oui.* 'Maybe I'll be a poet,' he says, 'instead of a lawyer.' "

And now all of it comes to Hannah, how he has gone to university, and his mother and father do not know of Hannah; they would not approve. She is Jewish, of course they would not approve, they being English, living in the country, his father a barrister. It is a bitter thing.

I can't care what they think, Russell says. You are the world to me, Hannah.

"I met someone this year who loves poetry," the girl says softly, raising her head to look at Hannah. "It's so difficult, though. He's not right, not right at all."

Hannah searches inside herself for something to say. Love is difficult, *bien sûr*. Yet one must have love in any case. The world is terrible enough without it, in spite of its beauty: this light, this day, the trees burning yellow, gold, the white bird swinging past the window. *Sometime too hot the eye of heaven.*

"One must—" Hannah begins. "The world—"

The girl comes so close Hannah can feel her breath.

"The world?"

"What are you two talking about?" The woman with the silver line in her reddish hair pokes her head in the door. She's drying a cup.

"Oh, just stuff." The girl jumps up and tosses her hair. She is a young woman, really, Hannah decides.

The woman looks at the young woman as if she is about to say something.

"God, my hair's a mop!" the young woman says. A horn beeps outside, and she rushes to the front window.

"Hodge is here!"

Hannah's thoughts scatter like feathers; what had she and the girl been saying? Words swirl, disappear. A young man carries grocery bags through the front door, the lovely girl rushes to the kitchen and back (*what is it she said? Hannah could feel her breath on her cheek*). The woman says to be quiet because Fiona's sleeping, the young man cries, "Happy birthday, Mir! I brought you a chocolate cake!" and then comes to Hannah and kisses her on the cheek.

"Hello, Hannah! I'm glad to see you. Have you seen Seamus yet? Have you seen the baby yet?"

How surprising! The day holds such delight. Yet something has saddened Hannah. Something is about to be said— oh, what is it? *The boy says, listen to this one, Hannah! She looks at his face as he reads, in the torchlight. Such a face must prove God's existence, in spite of the world's crumbling.*

And she held a baby once, in a cold place. It cried, without a father. Rough winds do shake.

"He's cute, isn't he?"

Hannah tries to smile. *Thou art more lovely.* She must know this kind young man, who kisses her, and who smells of leaves and smoke.

A baby cries—*aaah! aaah!* So sad, it sounds.

"Oops, that would be him! I'll be right back." Before Hannah can say a word, the young man darts out of the room.

"Ida! Can you help me with these bags?" the woman calls from the kitchen. "Ida?" But no one answers.

"Is Ida in here?" the woman asks, standing in the doorway, puzzled. "I thought she was with you, Mom. You're in here by yourself? Ida!"

And now a young man comes into the room, holding a baby. Wasn't he in a wedding? They took pictures. Hodge— wasn't that his name? Yes, Hodge—short for Roger.

"Hodge!" Hannah says.

"Yes? Would you like to hold Seamus for a minute, Hannah?" The young man—is it Hodge? And whom did he marry?—brings the baby close. How extraordinary! Could he really be giving this baby to Hannah? It settles into the circle of her arms, just like that. The young man sits right beside her and holds the baby's tiny hand.

It comes to her now, as in a dream: How could she not have realized? This baby is hers! Of course it is, hers and Russell's, not in a cold place now, with nurses brisk and unkind, and not on a huge boat, rising slowly and horribly up

59

and down, up and down, waves empty to the horizon. No; her baby is right here in her arms, on a sunny day.

The room sings with this knowledge, and more: how this young man, smiling at this baby, this is the one she loves, Russell Pearl, who held her in the frightening darkness, who made toast in the milky English light. How could she have believed he had vanished?

"I am so glad you are here," Hannah says to Russell.

"Thank you! I'm glad you could come today, Hannah. It's great to have two birthdays to celebrate."

Her baby will have a father; Hannah will not have to walk out of the hospital on her own, to stay in a room somewhere while she is still bleeding from the birth; she will not have to ask her cousin to send her money for the boat; she will not need to go across the ocean to Brooklyn, New York, or any other American place; she will live in England now, and the baby (*Miranda! of course, of course*) will grow up, and follow Hannah up the stairs, down the stairs; the nights will be peaceful, and the mornings too.

"I knew you would come back."

"Well, I was just at Stop and Shop, so it wasn't too hard to get here!"

How cheerful Russell is! Of course he is; the baby is safe and all of them are alive. *That one missed us, Hannah.* And now, soon, they will marry. Together, with this small one, they will make a family. Hannah has no family now but this.

"Look!" she says. "Look how beautiful!" The child's hair is feathery, the child's face is a soft moon.

"Yep, he's quite the boy! Not much of a sleeper, though."

"Where were you?"

Russell looks surprised.

"I was just out shopping, Hannah. I'm sorry I missed you earlier."

"I have missed you so much. Look at our baby!"

Russell looks at her sharply.

"I've missed you too, Hannah. This has been quite a week!"

Of course. He has been flying his plane, fighting the beasts. Yet, no, is the War not finished now? Is it not peacetime? If peace is possible. And perhaps, if Russell is here, the others will come soon.

Yet something is not right. *Summer's lease.* How does the poem go?

"Are you happy now?" she asks Russell. "To see our baby? Remember how you wanted to call her Miranda? And here she is—Miranda! Mir! I have waited so long for you to come and see her!"

Russell scratches his head.

"Wow, Hannah." He looks at her. Is he shy? she wonders. How is he shy with her? *Come with me to the bed, Hannah. Come now; I can't wait any longer.* Yet now he is shy and distant. He looks away.

A woman with silver in her hair comes into the room.

"Hodge, have you seen Ida?"

"Um . . . I think she's outside, talking on her cell phone."

The woman looks out the window. "Ah." She stands there for a moment. Then she starts to walk toward the kitchen. She hesitates at the doorway.

"Is Mom OK?"

"Well, yes, I think so. We've been having quite a conversation."

"Oh, really?"

The woman comes closer to Hannah. She bends toward her.

"Mom, you look tired. I can hold Seamus for you now."

The woman reaches her arms out for the baby, yet Hannah cannot give Mir up, of course not! Where will this woman take her!

The woman's hands slip under Mir's head, Mir's bottom. Hannah must do something. Cannot Russell see what is happening? He will not let the nurse take this little one away. Hannah has lost too much. She cannot lose this one too.

"Here we go, my little one!"

"Mais non!" Hannah cries. "This is our baby! You may not take her! Russell, do not let her do this!"

The room is very quiet. The woman stares at Hannah, her mouth open. She holds the baby against her shoulder. She looks frightened. What has frightened her? It is Hannah who is frightened!

"Mom, this is Hodge's and Fiona's baby, Seamus. It's not yours. I'm your child, if you can only remember! I'm Mir—Miranda! You gave birth to me in 1945, in England, and here I am, all fifty-five years of me, with you and your granddaughters, and Hodge—in Connecticut! My birthday's in two days, remember? I was born in October." She looks at Russell and says quietly, "Hodge, could you take

62

the baby? I think I should just sit with my mom for a moment."

"Of course." Russell stands up and plucks the baby out of the woman's arms. For a moment, Hannah is glad, yet before Hannah can think, he has vanished through the doorway, the baby too, just as he vanished once *in a meadow, on top of a cliff, the English Channel crashing in waves far below; he is ahead of her, walking, walking, and the sky is blue, and he looks over his shoulder, pointing at something—a bird, is it?—Hannah! he calls, Look! And then he walks into the blueness and is vanished; Hannah calls for him in terror, and the sky is blue and not a cloud in sight.*

Hannah's cheeks are wet.

A woman is sitting close to Hannah. She takes Hannah's hand and holds it in both her own. What is this sadness? What is it that has happened? Why does Hannah feel as if the sun has dimmed and all the world is only shadows?

"Do you remember the cake you used to make for my birthday?" The woman squeezes Hannah's hand.

Hannah shakes her head. Can there be cakes in such a world? Piles of corpses. Hannah does not think so.

"You would bake a torte, pure chocolate with cherries in it, so rich! I liked frosting, so you would make frosting too, even though you liked powdered sugar better. And you would write my name on top of the frosting in white letters: *Miranda.*"

Slowly, slowly, Hannah comes out of the shadows. Is she in a room, now? Sun comes at a slant onto the floor. The woman is talking of cakes. A little white goat.

And it is a lovely thing now, a gift, how Hannah can pic-
ture a little girl in a bright kitchen, leaning on her elbows,
watching Hannah as she ices a cake. The child has friends
over; Hannah has blown up balloons, for this child (Mi-
randa!) is an American child, and loves all things American.
Hannah is amazed, how she runs in the garden, how she
opens her presents so happily. After all, she is all right; some-
how Hannah has reached this place with her; somehow Han-
nah has made a home for her. It is difficult, yet sometimes
happiness enters in a rush of light, as if through a doorway
one had not known was there.

"Mom?" The woman is sitting close to Hannah on a couch. She is holding Hannah's hands in her own.

But thy eternal summer shall not fade.

A girl is standing in front of them. She looks like a slender bird, about to take flight. *thy eternal*

The woman is asking if the girl will stay for lunch. Does she have to go somewhere?

The girl looks at the floor for a moment, and then she looks up and says no, no, she will stay, her friend can wait, maybe she'll just forget about her friend. This is more important. The woman looks happy and relieved; she touches Hannah's arm.

Nor shall Death brag thou wand'rest in his shade

"Mom, let's have some lunch. And then we'll have a cake."

"Is it my birthday?"

The girl's face brightens. She laughs.

"Every day is your birthday, Grandma!"

"Your birthday's in March, remember? This is October. It's my birthday soon, and it's also the baby's; he was just born five days ago."

It is lovely to think of a baby, her hair all feathers. Can children mend the world?

As Hannah rises, with the woman's help, and starts to walk with the silver—thing on wheels—the girl arches her arms to put up her hair ("I'll come in a minute; I want to find the poem I wrote for Grandma, about her and Russell Pearl, meeting in the tea room"), and Hannah remembers a child who stood in front of her to give her a poem; another child who sang a song about sandwiches. She remembers a garden with daffodils along the walk, and another garden, the one where Auguste sleeps on the stone wall.

In this kitchen, all is bustling, plates coming out of cabinets, the refrigerator opening, bread being sliced, juice being poured. Outside the window is a sea of yellow, and, in the far distance, between two houses, past bushes and cars, Hannah glimpses a thin line of something beautiful. As she stands at the window, over the sink, she thinks of her own birthday, *her seventh; she is Hannah Luce, and she's in the garden with Maman and Tante Louise, and Emma, and Papa too, and the day is bright blue, in the cherry tree above her head, filled with white blossoms. Maman gives her a plate with a piece of her almond cake, and as Hannah takes her first mouthful, she thinks to herself, this is what I must write about, now, soon, for I am a poet, and the world is a poem—such a surprising thought to have, when you're seven, and all is still before you, England and America, the perishing of those you love, the baby crying on the boat, birthday cakes with balloons, a little girl running in a garden, a little girl coming out of the shadows of a pine tree. Here in this garden, you are seven years old and all of it is still to come.*

BABY-SITTER

$\mathcal{F}$iona McCarthy looks in the rearview mirror at her baby, Seamus, who catches her eye and waves wildly, as if swatting away a swarm of gnats. He grins, his gums a sweet pink, his eyes crinkling over some joke only a baby could understand. Fiona has just nursed him; he always finds the world a splendid place after a good milky snack.

"Hello, you," Fiona says, "Seamus the Great. So where do you think this road is, in all this snow?" Fiona glances at the paper in her hand. "Beach Rose. Miles from the beach, yes? Beached, maybe, in the middle of January." Beached, bleached, Fiona thinks, and soon she's thinking about the poems her sister, Ida, has written: pretty nice actually, all about sailing and love and drowning, and Pompeii, and bombs falling out of the sky, and Grandma Hannah crossing first the English Channel and then (with a baby!) the At-lantic. Ida's lucky to have her writing. Fiona's watercolors and oils languish in boxes under a table now, her art room (her bedroom, actually) usurped by her graphic design projects. Art changes when you have customers. And how on earth could I have thought I would just breeze along with such a business once the baby came? A baby (here Fiona slows for a small green sign, BEACH ROSE, and turns right carefully, because of the ice, onto a small street lined with older ranch houses and capes, their roofs laden with snow, a few valiant and bedraggled snowmen on front lawns), a baby is a much bigger change than she had known.

"One thirty-seven," says Fiona. "Help me look for it, Seamus."

Seamus waves and chortles. Fiona has the thought she has each day, a wish more than a thought: she pictures staying home with Seamus as other women in her neighborhood do with their small children, going for walks, doing the laundry, taking them shopping. Well, I do the laundry anyway, and I take Seamus for walks, and I shop with him, too, since Hodge is so busy as an editor for the town newspaper. How did her own mom take care of her and Ida and run a household and also work full-time at the museum? Of course, she was often exhausted; she would be so tired, having worked all day long, and then cooking dinner. And Grandma Hannah too had always worked, teaching high school French and English; she'd had to, being on her own. She wrote poetry, a wonderful thing in its way, but how much more could she have done? And why didn't she ever marry again?

The lure for Fiona is the notion of being cut loose from her business entirely for a while. She's only twenty-five. Some of her friends are still studying, and some have babies. She knows young women in her town on the Connecticut coast who live in nice houses already, without jobs, although how they can manage on one income Fiona has no idea. Newspapers certainly don't pay much. Fiona pictures a calm life, a beautiful life, filled with her art and baby socks and picture books and Seamus's smile. A simpler life, like in one of those paintings by Berthe Morisot. Of course, she and Hodge couldn't afford it, and still live in a town like this one, a place people in cities think of as a summer resort, with beach houses and historic buildings, quiet wealth and high costs. As it is, they can only rent the tiny house a few blocks from the beach, a two-bedroom.

She can't complain; whenever she thinks about how small her house is, she remembers Grandma Hannah, cooped up in her small room in assisted living at Tikkun, in the neighboring town, having had to move out of her sunny one-bedroom apartment in the prettier part of the building. And God knows what's next, thinks Fiona as she slows for an icy patch.

Fiona feels worried about the woman she's coming to see, the seventh one who's offered to care for Seamus five hours a day. There was the brusque older woman whose myriad of small charges looked like woeful prisoners in their playpens; the young mother of two boys whose house had very little in it but a couch and a kitchen table, and whose unfenced yard looked slippery with mud and old pieces of siding, even an old rabbit hutch with barbed wire; the woman who wished for better pay than her day-care job, but who hardly glanced at Seamus; the woman who screeched at her own children right in front of Fiona, frightening Seamus so much that he cried; the woman Fiona almost hired, who moved suddenly to Florida to start a new life; and the teenager Fiona actually hired for a week in November, through a nanny agency, for much too much money, who could think of nothing more to do with Seamus than to watch TV talk shows for hours, and who claimed she could not come on rainy days, because she'd had an accident once in the rain. Of course, she couldn't come on snowy ones either. Oh, and earlier Ida had offered, while Fiona was still pregnant, to help care for the baby for a whole year when it came, but that was before she graduated from college and decided on a whim to go to France.

Ida is so free, Fiona thinks, aware of her own wish, some days, to pop the baby in her mom's arms and sail somewhere astonishing: the Greek isles, Brazil. You're such a homebody, Fiona chastises herself; Ida has always had the courage to be independent. Off she goes, landing a job in Paris at the *Herald Tribune*, living in an apartment in the Marais, traveling to England with a friend. "You have to come visit, Fi! You'd love the galleries in London especially!" Fiona has yet to visit any part of Europe; she and Hodge can only afford day trips these days, to Mystic, to Newport; a year ago they camped in Maine. On their honeymoon they went to Montreal and could almost imagine they were in France. She has covered her refrigerator with the colorful postcards Ida has sent. One is of Rouen, the city Grandma Hannah lived in as a girl with her sister Emma. One is of Regents Park in London, another of a bombed-out cathedral—Coventry. One is of a beach somewhere, Fiona can't remember. Is Ida doing all this traveling alone? She never discusses her romantic life with Fiona; only sometimes Fiona guesses Ida has someone in the wings, most likely someone not right for her or why would she be so secretive? She is a bit unlucky in love, Fiona gathers. Maybe it's because she's so dramatic, takes everything so seriously; it could be hard, living with all that on a daily basis. Even Hodge is intimidated by Ida, and around him she's been on pretty good behavior.

On one postcard, Ida wrote, *I want to write better poems. The subject of Grandma Hannah still pulls at me. I want to understand what she suffered, to imagine her life from the inside out. I know so little about her. Do you know what I mean, Fi?* So like Ida, to write of such large subjects in such a small space. In another, with a picture of a bustling market in an old section of Paris, Ida described an afternoon she spent in the place where Jews were rounded up and shipped off to terrible deaths, children too. Fiona contemplates these pictures while she nurses Seamus in the kitchen.

And what can be said about all that? thinks Fiona now, following the curve of the road. Why is Ida so insistent about such things? Couldn't there be an end to the suffering now? Europe is more than the place where the Holocaust happened! Grandma Hannah lost so much—her sister, her whole family, her country—and yet she must agree, because Fiona cannot remember one conversation in which she spoke of sad things. On the other hand, there were her poems, which Fiona used to sneak looks at with Ida sometimes. Ida would read them out loud, with a hush in her voice, as they sat on the floor of Grandma Hannah's bedroom, with the door closed, and Fiona would try at first to understand the words, yet really she could never understand poetry. A poem about glass shattering, or a field in England—what could such poems be about? Ida would say she felt shadows in them, but Ida always said things like that. Fiona used to gaze at the old black-and-white photographs buried in Grandma's drawer. One she especially liked, of an older girl and a younger one on a bench under a tree, a fat white cat sitting between them. That must have been Hannah and Emma.

Fiona wishes for Seamus to know only happiness. If he likes poems, that will be fine, but she pictures him always in a beautiful and healthy place, as he grows up—a town with a beach, maybe, like the one near their house, curving around to the gray-green rocks, and with Little League, and a sweet shop on the small main street. How much trouble can a child get into in a town like this? Of course, even here, Fiona has to admit, terrible things happen; the synagogue was desecrated just a couple of years ago, its doors covered with Nazi signs and slogans in red paint. It is frightening to think about such things.

Fiona follows the bend of the road. Beach Rose must be a circle, she realizes, as she continues to the right. The houses here look well-tended. Along the left, the odd numbers: 129, 133, 135—137, a ranch of dull green. A golden retriever comes sauntering out from behind the house as Fiona pulls the old white Toyota onto the shoveled gravel driveway. In the front yard, a circle of stones surrounds a statue of the Virgin, painted blue and gold and white, her head and shoulders still covered in snow as she holds her hands out in blessing or dismay.

The conversation by phone with this woman, Zoe (here Fiona checks the sheet of paper to make sure she has the name right)—Zoe Corda—went well at first. She sounded intelligent and talkative, a good combination, Fiona thought, and she had a college degree. She had been hoping for just such a situation, caring for one baby in her own home. Fiona mentioned that actually she'd been hoping to find someone to come in, even though her own house was so small, instead of having to take the baby to a sitter's house, and that was when Zoe had told her about her condition. She had been in a wheelchair all her life—she was now thirty-five—but she knew this would present no difficulty in taking care of a baby.

Fiona had hesitated. She had pictured Seamus falling on his head, slipping off this woman's lap, or toddling around, once he could walk, and getting into all kinds of mischief and danger, and how would someone in a wheelchair be able to catch him?

"I'm studying for a degree in nursing," Zoe had added.

"Ah!" Fiona had said. There had been an uncomfortable pause.

"A lot of people think that just because I'm in a wheelchair, I can't take care of children."

Fiona listened.

Zoe continued, "And that just isn't true. I can do as well—I can do better than most people could. I can walk, actually, for a certain amount of time each day, with my leg braces and my crutches. I've taken courses in early childhood development, too."

What Fiona had wished to say was something blunt and honest, like "What will you do if my baby slips off your lap?" But something in this woman's voice, some determination, even sternness, had made Fiona think, maybe she's right, and how can I know unless I visit her in her house? Of course, this was precisely what Zoe urged her to do.

"You wouldn't believe how many people just say no to me, just like that, over the phone, before they've even met me. I don't think that's fair, do you?"

"No," Fiona had said, suddenly quite sure of this. The world is unjust, she had thought, and am I to be part of such injustice?

Fiona opens her car door gingerly, trying to ignore the golden retriever, who stands two feet away, tail wagging slowly. He comes closer to sniff her rubber boots and her jeans as she opens the back door of her car to unbuckle Seamus from his car seat. She's a little afraid of dogs, ever since her childhood, when a boxer pushed her down in New Haven and she smacked her head on the sidewalk. Grandma Hannah had been walking with her then, and was beside herself with distress; Fiona had had to comfort her, standing up quickly to show her she was all right. You had to be careful with Grandma. Ida always tipped her over the edge, made her upset about something, like the night Grandma was baby-sitting, and Ida wouldn't come in. Grandma Hannah just stood on the porch and cried. Fiona heard her, after she finished practicing one of her pieces on the piano; she hovered by the screen of the front door, unsure what to do. When Ida showed up, Fiona wanted to wring her neck.

"Good dog," she says nervously. "Just stay away."

She pulls the diaper bag over her shoulder as she lifts Seamus out, careful not to bump his head—something she did a few days ago in haste. His forehead still has the bruise, small and yellowish, just under his fine hair.

Walking up to the front door, arms full with Seamus, Fiona almost slips on the first step. Someone has shoveled the walkway and the steps, but the ice is thin and difficult to see. Fiona tightens her hold on her baby and rings the doorbell.

"Here we go, Captain," Fiona says, aware of an impulse to walk right back down the icy steps and plump Seamus into his car seat, pull out of the driveway and follow Beach Rose to its opening. She waits for half a minute, her toes becoming colder as Seamus soberly studies the shiny handle on the outer storm door, and then the front door opens. Fiona looks through the storm door at a small woman in a wheelchair, her thin legs like popsicle sticks. At her side is a patient-looking yellow Labrador.

"Come in," the small woman says brusquely, and Fiona pulls open the storm door and steps onto the mat in the front hallway, well away from the dog. She is grateful he doesn't sniff her. The mat has a picture of two border collies on it, and the words, *Welcome to our Home*.

"You're Fiona McCarthy?" the woman asks.

Fiona smiles. "Yes, I'm Fiona, and this is Seamus. Actually, his whole name is Seamus Field. His last name is different from mine." She blushes, feeling foolish somehow, and nods at Seamus, who is gazing in awe at the shiny silver spokes and arms of the wheelchair. Spying the dog, Seamus waves wildly for a moment and makes a high-pitched squeal of greeting. The Lab looks up at him with mournful eyes.

"I'm Zoe Corda," says the woman, holding out her hand for Fiona to shake, which Fiona does, awkwardly, by moving Seamus over to her left arm and giving Zoe her right hand. "Of course, I must be!" she adds. "I'm the only one here in a wheelchair!"

Fiona smiles uncomfortably. In the dimness of the hallway, she can't fully see the woman's face as she offers this joke. Her hair looks dry and wispy, reddish blond and almost reaching to her shoulders. Fiona can tell Zoe uses curlers, because round puffy waves surround her thin face.

Fiona thinks suddenly of her Great Aunt Trudy, her dad's aunt, in West Roxbury, an old Irish woman, confined to a wheelchair in her fifties, her smile recklessly lopsided from a stroke. She smoked Kools on the good side of her mouth, and coughed with phlegmy gusto into Kleenexes. As a child, Fiona had felt shy and miserable each time her family had visited Aunt Trudy in her apartment that smelled like something rotting. "Come here and give us a kiss," Trudy would say, and Fiona would go, because her mom would be pushing her between her shoulder blades. Fiona and Ida wouldn't linger, though, or talk much to Aunt Trudy; it had been hard to understand her, and it had been terrible to watch her tongue roll around in her mouth like that. She and Ida would giggle until their mom told them to hush.

Zoe shows Fiona the house she lives in with her father and her two dogs. Jack's the golden, and the Lab is Haven, because her father found him on a street in New Haven, cowering beside a dumpster.

"Haven and I have the house to ourselves all day," Zoe says as she touches the button that propels her wheelchair forward. She shows Fiona first the living room, decorated with gold drapes and gold patterned slipcovers on a couch and chairs, and then the dining room, where artificial flowers sit in a vase on the table. A piece of embroidery has been framed and hung on the wall—a picture of Saint Francis, with birds on his hands and at his feet.

Haven walks patiently beside the wheelchair. When Zoe pauses, Haven pauses. When she says "sit," Haven sits on his old haunches until she says "up."

"He helps me with all kinds of things," Zoe says, showing Fiona how Haven can open the fridge, or fetch anything he can hold in his mouth. When Zoe asks him to bring her his ball, Haven lopes under the table to fetch a big cloth ball, a faded blue, walking back to drop it into Zoe's lap. As soon as she tosses it into the kitchen, Haven careens after it with astonishing speed. He brings it back to Zoe and sits in front of her with hope.

"Up," says Zoe. "Come on," and Haven and Fiona follow her into the kitchen, a slightly brighter room with yellow walls, tidy and clean. From the kitchen, Zoe brings Fiona to a sunny room—a glassed-in porch, with a couch and wicker chairs, ivy and fragrant narcissi on the windowsill, a few books on a shelf, a TV, photographs in frames.

"This is the room I'm in most of the day," Zoe says. She looks at Fiona straight-on. Fiona is startled by her eyes, sharp blue and keen. She feels young and somehow inept in front of this small, fierce woman.

Seamus begins to wriggle in Fiona's arms. His face is pink with the effort to shed his fuzzy yellow snowsuit. Fiona perches on the couch, laying him on his back and unzipping his suit, untying the laces under his chin, and pulling off his hood and then the little cotton cap, the one her mother gave him, so that his soft blond hair stands up wildly all over his head.

"So—this is where I would take care of your baby," Zoe says, looking finally at Seamus. Fiona can sense Zoe staring at him, as she gently pulls first one plump arm out of the suit, then the other, then each of his sturdy legs. Something in her face reminds Fiona uncomfortably of Ida; Ida seems so drawn to Seamus, yet so bothered by his very presence. Fiona's mom thinks Ida is jealous, and maybe this is true; Fiona does not like to inspire jealousy, has tried to avoid causing it all her life. And what does Ida have to be jealous about, anyway? She's very pretty, and very resourceful. She's twenty-three years old and having a blast in France, for heaven's sake. Surely she'll marry one day, and have children, if that's what she wishes. It's not Fiona's fault if she doesn't.

Seamus's diaper is wet, and Fiona opens her diaper bag on the floor, holding on to Seamus with her right hand as he squirms and kicks, beginning his intricate trilling sounds—his song, as Fiona thinks of it. Seamus loves songs. Fiona sings to him all the time; his favorite is the Yiddish one Grandma Hannah taught Fiona when she was a child, about a little goat. Once, a couple of weeks ago, Grandma Hannah started to sing, too; Fiona had been so happy to hear her, she'd found her eyes filling and she hadn't been able to continue.

Fiona pulls the tabs on Seamus's diaper. Sometimes Grandma Hannah makes Fiona's neck tingle when she forgets who Seamus is—and Fiona too. She had not thought her grandma—always with sweets in her purse for Fiona and Ida, always with a kiss for each cheek (strict too, though, and impatient sometimes)—could ever forget her. Hannah recently has begun to call Fiona Mir, and she sometimes calls Seamus Mir, too. When Ida came home to Wethersfield in December to celebrate Christmas and Hanukkah, Grandma Hannah thought she was her sister Emma! Ida took it with grace, actually; after a few minutes, she stopped trying to correct Hannah's mistake. Grandma Hannah acted as if it were the most natural thing in the world for her sister to be twenty-three years old and American. Of course, Ida cried later; Fiona found her sitting next to O'Hearn in the den, scratching him behind the ears, her eyes red, her face puffy and wet.

It doesn't bear thinking of, Fiona says to herself now, her hand on Seamus's belly. Seamus smiles at Fiona radiantly, as she lifts him to slip the new diaper under his soft bottom. She hopes he doesn't pee, as he often likes to do; it must be the splendid feeling of air on his skin, so covered always, that inspires him. She covers him up again quickly, and slips back on the legs of his yellow jumper. He kicks the air as if he's riding a bicycle to the sky. Hodge calls him the Sky-Flier.

Lifting Seamus from the couch, Fiona holds him under his arms, facing Zoe. His small feet touch her knees and push as Seamus bounces crazily. Zoe looks at him with a stiff smile on her face; it occurs to Fiona that she may be out of the habit of smiling.

"Are you—" in pain, she almost asks, but something in Zoe's face makes her think better of it.

"Would you like to hold him?" she asks instead.

"OK," Zoe says, so hungrily that Fiona chastises herself for not thinking to ask sooner. Fiona carefully places Seamus on Zoe's lap, where he sits, rounded, Zoe holding him under his arms, and he hunches contentedly, gazing at her face.

"So you're Seamus," she says.

At this, Seamus's arms start to flap. Zoe smiles at him, a small smile, almost tender. For a moment, she looks younger, and Fiona almost forgets about the wheelchair, bigger than Zoe herself, and about her worries. Isn't it just love I want, for Seamus? she thinks.

With Seamus on her lap, Zoe talks about getting her degree in nursing, which she hopes to use, although it's difficult to find a position as a nurse when you come with a wheelchair. She talks about this room, how it's perfect for a small child, big enough to run around in, and of course she would have lots of toys and things for Seamus to do. Fiona listens, and tries to picture Seamus here on his own with Zoe.

"Would you be able to take him outside?" she asks.

Zoe hesitates. For the first time she looks unsure of herself. "Well, my father could maybe make a fenced-in area, you know, with a sandbox and maybe a swing."

Fiona stands up and looks out the window at the large, unfenced yard out back. She sees the dog Jack lying on a cleared area of the back deck. A wooden ramp goes off the deck.

"So—" Fiona worries about how her question will sound. "You go out yourself?" she asks, nodding at the wheelchair.

"Oh, yes, I go out," Zoe says, indignant. "I can drive."

Fiona pictures Seamus, a plump boy of two, on chunky legs, slipping around to the front of the house and standing smack in the middle of the road, as her neighbor's two-year-old likes to do. One summer dusk, when Fiona came home in her Toyota, the little girl simply stood right in front of her driveway, looking at her headlights. How can you keep a child safe in this world?

"I like him to play outside each day," Fiona says, rubbing her elbows, aware of her worry rising.

"I would take him out," Zoe says, yet Fiona does not feel reassured.

"I would teach him," Zoe adds, "about safety. I wouldn't let him do anything unsafe." She looks at Seamus as she talks, and he reaches for her face. She's in love already, thinks Fiona. How quick it is. She begins to feel she should bring Seamus here, for Zoe's sake.

As Zoe tells Fiona how her father would put a crib right by the window, and make the side come down easily for her, so she can reach for the baby, Seamus starts to open his mouth and nod toward Zoe's small chest. His tongue, pink as a shell, rolls wetly. Fiona is quickly aware of the fullness of her breasts, aching with the urge for Seamus's mouth, his insistent suck. Her milk lets down in a wet trickle. Within a matter of seconds, Seamus begins to wriggle in Zoe's hands, his face flushed, the small whimpers beginning as he becomes aware of his hunger. Zoe looks at Seamus in dismay, and then at Fiona.

"I think he's getting hungry," Fiona says, feeling her bra now wet with milk, her own hands itchy for Seamus.

A glimmer of something enters into Zoe's face—disappointment, is it, or fury? Something else, too: yearning, yearning as pure and sharp as Seamus' for Fiona, as Fiona's for Seamus. It occurs to Fiona that she has seen this look on Grandma Hannah's face sometimes.

"Do you have a bottle?" Zoe asks. "I can feed him." Her voice has acquired a panicked edge, as if this loss of him to Fiona heralds a larger loss. And perhaps it does, Fiona thinks, as she shakes her head, feeling the heat of a blush on her face.

"I'm nursing him, actually. That's something I would need to talk to you about."

Fiona rises and plucks Seamus, sobbing now, out of Zoe's lap. As she walks back to the couch, she begins to unbutton her shirt, and before she's even sitting, Seamus has his mouth on her right breast. As he sucks, tightly and fiercely, the milk drips from her other breast, and soon she switches Seamus to this one, to relieve the fullness. She watches his delicate face, his eyes swooning, his fingers caressing her breast and her shirt.

"You see, I was actually looking for someone to come in," Fiona says.

"Couldn't you start him on a bottle during the day?" Zoe looks older again, the radiance washed from her face.

Fiona blushes. "Yes, I would have to. I would try to express some milk for him each day, and bring the bottles to you."

As she says this, though, Fiona feels ridiculous here in this woman's house, and more than ridiculous—at fault. *I will never let Seamus stay here*—this thought hovers in the air of the room, stubborn and merciless.

Seamus pulls more slowly now at her breast. His swoon changes, before Fiona's eyes, into sleep. In a moment his mouth loosens its hold and her nipple pops out. Seamus's mouth continues to suck, and he lifts his head slightly, as if to catch her breast again, but then he relaxes into her arm, his mouth a tight bud.

Zoe is talking now—something about how much she reads, how she would read picture books to Seamus daily— but Fiona can't listen, overwhelmed as she is with a familiar ache, in the form of a small ghost, hovering just out of her vision, near the crook of her elbow where Seamus's head lies cradled. Emma, it is, yearning for something: a touch, a mother. She is composed of yearning. It comes to Fiona, as it always does, how Ida used to ask questions again and again of their mom, while Fiona, pretending to be occupied with something else, would act as if she couldn't care less, yet all the while she would listen with painful avidity; sometimes she felt strangely as if Ida spoke the questions for her.

Q. Why did Emma stay in France?
A. She had pneumonia.

Q. Why couldn't she just have gone with Grandma Hannah anyway? Didn't you say that friends in England helped them both get visas?
A. Yes, and she was supposed to go, but they couldn't bear to send her, especially once she came down with the illness.

Q. But didn't they know what would happen?
A. No one could know that, Ida. We've talked about this before. It must have seemed as dangerous to go as to stay.

Haven gives a loud sigh from his position on the rug by Zoe's wheelchair.

"Well," Fiona says. She fiercely wills the air around Seamus's fuzzy head to be clear—just air. And yet, she knows it's not so simple. A presence like this one can slip into the most unwelcome places: her and Hodge's bed, just as Hodge moves to kiss her; the faces of children in her neighborhood, gazing at her as she drives past; the shadows cutting into the gray-green rocks in the Sound; this house on Beach Rose, where the small woman in a wheelchair is staring at Fiona as if to pry out of her something valuable—a *yes*—a *this will be fine.*

"So," Fiona says, hesitant, unnerved.

Zoe looks at her sharply, stung already, knowing what's coming.

Fiona blushes again. "I'll think about this, and I'll call you in a day or two," she says, knowing that she'll procrastinate, that one day will spill into another, filled with tiredness and Stop and Shop and sandwiches for dinner, folding pile after pile of clothes and singing Seamus to sleep, walking in the cold air along the water, talking with Hodge, or quarreling, shoveling the snow off the sidewalk again, visiting Grandma Hannah, writing cheerful emails to Ida, and (yes) trying to ignore the ghosts hovering, one after the other, this one especially. Each day will come and go, bright and shadowy, joyful and disturbing, until Zoe will slip into that other world of memory, and Fiona will feel too guilty and too embarrassed to call.

Q. What happened to her?

Fiona lifts Seamus, still asleep, to her shoulder and covers him with his small yellow blanket. His round head sinks into her shoulder with soft weight. She should write to Ida tonight; she hasn't heard from her in almost three weeks.

A. I've told you. She died at a camp, at Drancy, in France. Remember, Grandma Hannah had a letter, from a friend in France, a neighbor? Someone got the letter to her. And also she looked at the lists, in Paris, after the War.

With one hand, Fiona stuffs Seamus's snowsuit and cap into the diaper bag, and then carefully she stands up, the bag's strap over her shoulder. Haven rises to his feet with a groan. Fiona decides to stop by the fish store on her way home.

"I'll call you soon," she says. Zoe pushes the button on her wheelchair. Fiona follows her, with Haven, to the front door and opens it, and then she opens the storm door. With a nod and a fleeting smile to Zoe, Fiona is outside.

The snow glitters sharply on the lawn. Fiona goes slowly down the steps and along the walk, Seamus still asleep on her shoulder. She can't wait to buy the fish, to glimpse the Sound as she crosses the little bridge over the tidal river, to enter her own small house, to kiss Hodge when he comes in the front door, to see the snow turn yellow and then pink, then dark purple, as she marinates the fish and cuts up red peppers and mushrooms, to nurse the baby in the rocking chair by the crib after supper, as Hodge washes the dishes and listens to jazz, to curl up with Hodge on the sofa in front of the TV, to slip into bed next to him after nursing the baby, her breasts still tingling. All she wishes for is an ordinary life, clear and touched with beauty. How is she hurting anyone else with such a wish?

Q. How did Emma die?
A. I don't know.

Q. Were her parents with her when she died?
A. I hope so.

Q. But why didn't she go with Hannah?
A. I told you all I know.

Looking over her shoulder as she walks to her car, Fiona sees Zoe in the dimness behind the front door. On Zoe's face is a look Fiona knows will haunt her in the coming years, a look of defeat and of a sorrow so immense it could not possibly be contained inside one person. Fiona imagines Zoe bound by ropes, like Odysseus, only she isn't simply Zoe, but Hannah too, and she hasn't asked to be lashed to the mast, she just is; and it isn't the Sirens' song she desires so intensely she would drown for it, it's this child asleep in Fiona's arms, dreaming of perfect happiness.

RESCUE

The circles of Hannah's silver walker go round and round, so quietly! Hannah holds on to the—silver things—and she's walking, walking, not inside, not in her room, with the girl with honeyed hair, needing brushing, not in the hallway near the pink—boxes—with women opening them and bringing out—documents—but outside, elsewhere! The trees wave to her, and people walk along with her. Oh, this is a day of surprise.

On the—place to walk—lie a few bits of glass (*non!*), ice! What is this season? Hannah looks up as she walks. Arms on the trees—how bare! Hannah shivers. This is the season of greatest quiet. Letters stop coming, until a letter comes to turn the world to ice.

The air is cold on her head, her shoulders. *Tiens!* Where is her coat? Hannah looks down. She has on—how puzzling!— her blue sweater. It is a little warm, not warm enough. She pauses to look at the buttons; yes, the buttons have been put right. But how odd, *quand même!* Is this a dream? Too cold for a dream! She slips her hand into the pocket. In any case, she has her Kleenex. And in the basket on her silver wheeled—is her purse.

Hannah is astonished, how much she can walk. One foot goes forward, then the other. The glass (*non!*), the glittering stuff glints.

Cars go along, both ways. House after house after house. Wet gardens, nothing much yet. Walking, walking, and now a park, big and with bits of green, across the street. Trees stretching, gray, white, black, higher than the houses all in a row, higher than the shops, almost as high as the point of the church. Hannah is in America, of course she is, close to—home, she is sure. If only she can figure out which way to go. Oh! She must try not to become too tired.

An alarm sounds, quickly: *dring, dring!* Hannah holds on to the silver handles. Swooshing past her, two bicycles, and on them, two boys. *Dring, dring!* Hannah tips to one side, but she holds on, and the boys cycle off. They have— packages—on their backs. Inside might be their papers. Hannah remembers that she teaches in a school. Our Lady of— Oh! How can she not know the Lady?

A yellow bus goes by. Maybe she should take a bus to the school (*Our Lady*). *Non!* She has a car, of course she must! How to know which is hers? In America, every family has one. One takes the bus in—other places; one takes the train. Hannah must not think about trains.

"Can I help you?"

Hannah is startled. She looks up at a girl in a coat and a scarf.

"Can I help you? Are you looking for something?"

Am I? wonders Hannah. She's missing so many things. If only she can think carefully, she will remember. This is the quiet season.

"Are you looking for the stores?"

"Yes," says Hannah, although she is unsure.

"Which store do you want?" The girl looks into Hannah's face. Hannah gazes at a whole row of shops across the street, along another edge of the park.

"The grocery store?" asks the girl. "Or maybe the drugstore?"

"The drugstore!" says Hannah, relieved to hear of something so familiar. Oh, she has been inside a drugstore. Once inside, possibly she will find what's missing.

"OK. Do you know which one it is?"

Hannah studies the shops. Some have big windows, with pine boughs all around. One has books. One has hearts in a row. One has toy animals—Hannah cannot see them well, yet she pictures a duck, a lamb. A little girl she knows—how does one call her?—would like such a toy. Do I have the right money? Hannah worries. If I have no money, I cannot buy a soft duck for the child.

"It's right there, next to the grocery store," says the girl. "See? It has red hearts in the window."

Hannah looks. Of course the drugstore has red hearts! Her confusion vanishes.

"*Merci beaucoup, mademoiselle.*"

The girl stares. "OK. Good luck," she says, and she gives Hannah a little wave.

It is difficult, knowing how to cross. Hannah forgets what the lights mean. A little person on the—a little person lights up in white. Hannah sees two cars halt. She waits.

One car honks its horn. Hannah looks inside the—car's glass. A woman is looking straight at her and waving her hand in the air. She looks impatient. Oh! The woman is unrolling her glass. She shouts something. Hannah feels uncertain about this day.

"Go ahead!" This is what she is shouting. "You can go now!"

Hannah is relieved. She had thought the woman was shouting something—other. She holds tight to her silver—and walks, slowly, slowly.

You must have courage to be out in the world, of course Hannah has always known this. She walks in front of the woman's car. Her wheels go round and round, all the way to the other—bank. Shore.

Now to cross another—where cars go and halt, go and halt. Only if she crosses can she enter the store with the hearts, pink, red, dancing in a row on the window. Hannah shivers. Her ears ache from the cold.

Perhaps it is on a day like this one that the world becomes unfamiliar for those Hannah loves. She has the letter still, from Mme Joupert, the kind neighbor who puts out milk for Auguste, and who greets Hannah daily. *(Bonjour, Hannah, ça va? Il fait beau aujourd'hui, n'est-ce pas?)* The first time she opens the letter, it is an early spring day,

96

in England, and she knows the wintry story is real; the world inside her is shattered. Yet soon all again is quiet, no letters coming, and Mme Joupert's letter begins to appear like a dream—perhaps true, and yet distant—a fiction, really, for how could it be so? If it is so, how can Hannah continue to live?

She waits for a minute, another, and another. Cars come, go, stop, go. All the people know how to stop, when to go. Only Hannah continues to wait.

A young man comes up to Hannah's spot on the sidewalk. He holds tight to a—chair with wheels. A baby is inside, all bundled up in a blanket the color of—Hannah does not know the word for the color. On the baby's head is a cap. The young man looks straight ahead, and then he glances at Hannah. He gives a little smile and a nod.

I must follow him, thinks Hannah. And, *voilà!* When a little white person is lit up, the young man starts to push the—rolling thing—across the street. He looks at Hannah once over his shoulder as if to say, Come along! Hannah comes along.

On this side, the shops look bigger.

Roundish, pale yellow vegetables sit in—big bowls. Bins. Inside the door is a table holding little green boxes of—small berries, red, the ones that hide close to the ground—how are they called? How could such fruit be here when it is so cold? A miracle. A woman carrying two big bags squeezes past her.

What is it Mme Joupert writes? Something too terrible for words.

"Are you heading in or out?" says someone at Hannah's

elbow—a man in a uniform, with white hair. He pushes past Hannah and goes into the shop.

Here people buy fruits, things for soup; they wheel babies and baskets. Hannah is not worried about a uniform. How could a family be taken—elsewhere? Of course this cannot happen; this happens only in dreams. *Ma chère Hannah, J'espère que tu es en bonne santé. J'ai quelque chose de difficile à t'écrire.* Something difficult to write. I hope you are in good health.

Is this the store she planned to enter? Hannah has doubts. She would like to buy those green leafy—and those yellow— She cannot remember all the words, but she can guess how each one would taste, in a soup, or with a— roast! Her mother teaches her how to make roasts. Yet how would she bring such food home? She lives now— doesn't she—in a place with pink boxes and a tree outside the window. And she cooks—where does she cook? It is too confusing.

Hearts. This is what the girl said. The drugstore has hearts in the window. How silly of me! thinks Hannah. This shop has no hearts pasted in a window, of course not.

Hannah's toes feel cold. She looks at her feet. *Tiens!* She has her slippers on. How odd. In her—home—her slippers keep her toes warm. But out here! One wears—something else, another color, not soft. She pictures the ones in her closet: shiny black ones that pinch her toes, others the color of caramel, with laces. It is the laced ones she wishes to have now, even though they are ugly. Someone promises to buy her new ones. That will be lovely. Her slippers are small and made of something like a towel. How is she wearing these outside, in this cold?

One is freezing, Hannah thinks, yet one goes on. How else is one to do it? *Ma chère Hannah. Le 14 janvier. Les gendarmes. Ton papa, dans son cabinet de médecine.* In his doctor's office. She begins to walk again, looking at her slippers. First one, then the other, goes forward.

And now, in front of Hannah, is a big window with hearts pasted in a row. Each one has a letter: H – A – P – P –Y – V – A – L – E –

Yes, Hannah knows this holiday, in America. She knows a child who makes hearts for her classmates, with paper lace and red paper. Carefully, the child writes each name, so much does she wish to please the others. The child is—Mir, of course she is.

Hannah knows now, with certainty, that she brought Mir to this country, where one has hearts, and not the stars sewn on. Hannah knows of such stars (*Juif* in black letters on a yellow star). She has seen pictures. She knows of such things. Yet to think that Emma, and *Maman.* Even *Papa.* And Rosalinde, who lives two houses up. And—Hannah can hardly think this, ever—*Grand-mère Aline* who lives just five houses away, and also *Grand-mère Erma,* in Paris. In the other country, where Hannah comes, people at least wear no stars. She can walk on the gray—places—take the underground, ring Russell's—little button by his door—and all the people cannot know who she, Hannah Luce, is. She looks like any ordinary person. When she thinks of her real country, sometimes she sees a zoo, and it is her family in the cages, with the yellow stars. People look at them—at all the people Hannah cares about—huddled in the cage. And then there is something more terrible.

A large door, all of glass, opens, and a young woman with a small child on her arm holds the door for Hannah ("Let's go home!" she says to the child), and Hannah pushes her silver—into the brightness and warmth.

Near Hannah is a row all of—papers. Red-and-white ones, with pictures of cartoons and balloons, make a pretty wall. Little signs, red, say HAPPY VALENTINE'S DAY, GRAND-MOTHER, GRANDDAUGHTER, MOTHER, DAD, WIFE, SON, FRIENDS, SISTER. LOVE. ROMANCE. BLANK.

The—papers—look cheerful and noisy. Hannah pictures herself buying a dozen of them, and mailing them—to whom? To her cousin Julianne—*non!* Is she still alive? Is she in a hospital? To a baby. To her friend, also French, who goes with Hannah to the movies, out for coffee—she has such a friend still, *non?* To her daughter, certainly. Hannah is sure she has a daughter, a beautiful baby—*non!* A beautiful girl, with blond hair.

Ma chère Hannah. Ta famille. Par le train à Drancy. Ta sœur, Emma. Un ami de ton papa m'a dit qu'elle était malade. Hannah cannot understand; how could her sister be taken to such a place? How could she grow sick? How could she not be breathing still?

It is like a dream now, coming, a dream Hannah knows, where she is reading a letter, and inside her becomes ice. Soon it is as if the ice blows apart, shatters, and Hannah is not sure what is left of her but—glinting slivers, all around. At the center, nothing.

Coming always with this dream, another: a list on a wall. Others crowd her; it is difficult to read the names. Is this a dream, or is this real? When she discovers certain ones, she knows she cannot live.

This is how the names line up now, in a row, sober and quiet. "Go!" she tries to say to them, "*Allez!*" yet her mouth is ice.

The first one: *Louise Nadel, amie.*

Non!

The second: *Aline Luce, grand-mère!* whose scent surrounds me.

The only way to save oneself, from the third, the fourth, is to look at something in the here and now, something small perhaps, but real. Hannah forces herself to turn to the other row of—leaves—*non!* papers—not red ones, other colors. Other words: FOR A NEW BABY. NEW HOME.

SYMPATHY.

But this is not enough.

Do others not hear this list? It goes on and on, merciless, yet filled with mercy too somehow, each name a prayer and also a shout, a cry, like those posted at the hotel in Paris, that Hannah makes herself search, after the—her heart in—pieces.

Rosalinde Houpert, mon amie.

Déborah Joseph, ma cousine, who plays in the garden.

Eva Joseph, who cries to play too.

Alexandre Joseph, who reads all afternoon.

Renée Emont, l'amie de ma mère.

A woman, old (how few are so old!) comes down the hall

101

in the hotel, as skinny as the—arms—of a bare bush in win-
ter. Mme Emont? *asks Hannah, searching her face. The*
woman shakes her head. Est-ce que vous êtes de Rouen? *The*
woman's eyes are muddy. Je suis de Lyon. Ah, pardon.
Arrivez-vous d'Auschwitz? Oui. Reconnaissez-vous cette
jeune fille, cette femme? Non.

Sarah Rothko.
Isaac Rothko.
Abraham Rothko.
Isabelle Berg.
Reconnaissez-vous la femme dans cette photo? Non.
Reconnaissez-vous cette famille? Elle est de Rouen, peut-
être tuée à Drancy ou Auschwitz. Non, désolée.
Henri Luce, mon oncle!
Nadine Luce, ma tante.
Benjamin Luce.
Cet homme?
Non.
Esther Luce.
Cette femme? Reconnaissez-vous?
Non.
Robert Luce.
Arrêtez!

The names go slowly at first, one by one, like ice people,
until they jostle each other and break and spill brightly and
coldly into the shop, and make a pool around Hannah, so
thickly they gather, cold water filled with bodies—a flood.
Some cling to Hannah's ankles and knees with hands like
twigs. In her ears is a rising noise. She closes her eyes, yet the

names continue to announce their presence, cling to her coldly.

Can she not stop this? Can she do nothing? She is nothing, then. She opens her eyes to bring this world in, not that one, yet it is merciless.

Daniel Luce, Papa!

Le monde est perdu. The world, lost.

Berthe Luce.

Tout est perdu. All, lost.

Em—

Someone cries out.

Hannah holds to the silver—hands. She cannot breathe well. She has shattered, utterly.

"Can I help you?"

The question is far off, abstract, impersonal.

"Excuse me, ma'am. Are you all right? Can I help you?"

Hannah opens her eyes. To her surprise, a woman is in front of her, wearing—glass—on her face, and a pink sweater. She has short blond hair, with brown at the bottom. She stares at Hannah with a frightened look, as if Hannah is a ghost. Hannah feels odd too, not herself at all, or as if her self has scattered, like cherries spilled from a basket, and yet here she is, something like bones and skin, but colder. The air is clear now, though, and the floor too, clear of icy hands pulling, and for this Hannah is grateful. Yet of course one must be ready for their return.

The woman looks impatient. What is it she wishes?

The woman says something more. Hannah knows this

103

language; she thinks it must make sense, yet the sounds are like the tapping of a bird's beak on a tree. If one cannot understand the words, one must study the face. Is she kind, or is she not kind? It is important to know. The woman's eyebrows are thin and crooked, as if painted on by a child; this may not be her fault, however. Hannah looks at her own hands on the silver—

"Il faut que je . . ." What is it Hannah must do? She looks around. Rolls of paper for wrapping presents stand in a row further down. What is it she wishes to buy?

"Where do you live? Can someone in the store help you get home?"

Ah! This language is clear. Jigsaw puzzle pieces come to Hannah: a tree with white blossoms, a bed in lamplight, blue and gray ocean to the horizon, gray streets, a kitchen with books and a girl at the table, little girls running in a garden, shadows under a pine tree. Yet all the names have gone.

"Do you know where you live?"

The woman's stare is not kind, Hannah decides.

It comes to her now: this is how one is captured; this is how one is pulled from all one knows, and put in—a cold place, a place to make one ill, to break a family into slivers. She thought this country was safe, yet no country is safe, of course not. Mme Joupert is kind, but other neighbors turn their heads, or whisper to an authority. The woman will say her name to the police; Hannah will be put on a list, to become a name spilling brightly, a cry, a something only, behind the papers. She will cling as the others cling. She will not walk here, in this country, on the— She will not go—home. This is how she has always known it would be, and now here it is. It is terrible.

"Listen, you can't do this in here," the woman with the blond hair says. "This is a store. You'll upset the other customers. You can't stand here crying. You have to let us help you get home."

Allez! the soldiers say, right in one's home, and push one to pack a bag, and a bag for one's children—what belongs to each? A sweater, a coat. *Vite!* to the station, and then onto the train, an ordinary train yet strange now, a prison; leaving one's house, one's self behind. The cat hides in the cherry tree or in the shadows under the bed. The soup is on the stove. The house is clean, the windows washed. It is winter. Inside the hard ground, crocuses sit, furled, tight, waiting for spring. The ivy in the window will need water; the cat will need milk. The child's books sit in a row on her shelf. How often has Hannah imagined this?

Hannah sits on the chair of her silver— Someone is making a terrible sound. Her hands touch her face and come away wet—with blood? *Non*—water.

The woman is talking. "Name," she says. "Please tell us your name."

What will happen if Hannah tells? What will happen if she refuses? Perhaps it is the same thing.

"*Non,*" she whispers. "*Je ne veux pas le dire.*" I do not wish to say my name.

"What?" The woman has her hands on her hips now. She is staring at Hannah.

"Je ne veux pas dire mon nom." I do not wish.

"Listen, ma'am, you've got to speak English. I can't understand you if you speak another language. You need some real help here."

Yes. Help me, thinks Hannah, *Au secours!* Yet the woman just sighs and shrugs.

"You stay right here. I'm going to get the manager."

Hannah watches the woman walk away fast. Her bottom shakes. She is a small, plump woman who is not used to difficulties. Perhaps now Hannah can escape.

As she pulls herself up and holds to the silver hands, starts to walk, a man comes to stand in front of Hannah. He is almost bald, with bits of brown hair, and he looks very tired. He is wearing a white shirt and a red—thing around his neck. He has a pen and papers in his shirt pocket, glasses on his nose. Not a police officer, Hannah is almost sure. Certainly not a soldier. Yet it is not always an official person who is most dangerous. He touches her elbow and bends to look into her eyes.

"Ellie tells me there's a little problem here."

A mother walks past, holding the hand of her little boy. The boy looks up at Hannah, his face open and surprised. "Come on," the mother says. She glances at Hannah and then looks away.

Hannah waits. What is it this one wishes her to say?

"Could you let me help you?"

Hannah looks at her hands.

"Is there someone who could come and help you? Do you have a family member in this area?"

Sometimes a person offers help, yet it is a mistake to say yes. One must be careful.

"A husband, maybe? A daughter or son? Who do you live with?"

Children too, *vite!* It doesn't matter how small, how frightened. Out of the house with them, to the—

"Can I see your purse for a minute? I'm just trying to figure out how to help you. Maybe there's a number in here, a name, someone to call?"

As he touches her purse, Hannah cries out.

"Well, I'm sorry. I just don't know what to do." The man rubs his bald head.

Two girls come near and look at the colorful papers. One of them looks at Hannah and then she chooses a paper in the row. "Listen to this one!" she says to her friend. "Steve would love this one." The girls bend their heads together and giggle.

"Emily?" the man almost shouts. "Em? Could you give me a hand over here?"

The girls both look over their shoulders and stare at Hannah, their eyes traveling over her coldly.

Now a new girl appears, her face lovely and questioning, and perhaps a little frightened.

"Em. Could you figure out how to—uh, encourage—this lady to open her purse and let you see some name, someone to call? I think she's lost. I've got too much going on right now to deal with this."

The girl, Em, smiles shyly at Hannah.

"Hi," she says.

Hannah tries to smile, yet this is difficult. She is very old, of course she is! It is not a simple thing to smile, when you are so old, and so worried.

The girl smiles and shrugs her shoulders.

"So . . . it's pretty cold out today, isn't it?"

"Oui, il fait froid."

"Oh, you speak French? I'm learning French in school."

Hannah looks at the girl's soft eyebrows, at the way her hair—bends, curves. Some survived, she is sure of this.

"Um, let me see . . . *Je m'appelle Emily.*"

Her name is Emily! Ah! How could Hannah not have known before? Is it possible? The joy rises and wrings Hannah's heart. Here, right here, in this place with the cards. Here she is, who is little, and who now is a girl in a T-shirt that says *Fish Tale Restaurant.* Right here, by the hearts. She has not perished—how could Hannah have believed this? Perhaps it is true, the terrible thing about *Maman et Papa,* and her cousins in Paris, even her *grand-mères,* who injured no one, yet it may not be true of all. A child could be ill, yet she could recover. She could be in an inhuman place of wire and muddy snow, caged like a small animal, yet she could escape. She is a good child, not spoiled; irritating only in the way little sisters are; she throws bits of her roll to the birds; she likes to draw; she likes to read. Someone would save her. Mme Joupert could save her! How could it be otherwise?

Hannah has such joy, she worries only that her heart cannot contain it. She holds out her hands, and the girl slowly puts hers into Hannah's.

"Tu es encore là. Je suis si heureuse, si—" Words fly away. How to say to Emma how happy she feels? How to help Emma feel at home here? She must have come far, all the way across the water.

"I—I'm not sure I understand. I think I know *heureuse*." The girl gently pulls her hands away. Oh, but it has been so long! Of course such an encounter is surprising; it breaks the world into little bits of color; it changes everything.

"Tu es en bonne santé? Tout va bien?" Hannah searches this face. Of course she would grow into such beauty! Here she is, her eyes bright, her hair clean and shiny, a young woman really. Such a face should not perish.

"Mon cœur," Hannah whispers. "I am so—sorry."

"Oh, don't worry! You shouldn't feel bad. You want to sit down?"

"I should have come home. I should have helped you get out. I did not know how it would be."

"I'm not sure what you . . ." The girl looks around, as if for help.

"Je suis tellement désolée." And this feeling, of being so very sorry, too sorry for words, fills this bright air now, and yet as it floats out, it vanishes. She could say this a thousand times, more than a thousand; she could say it each minute for the rest of her life, and still she would not have exhausted her urge to say this, and still all these sorries could not be enough, could not fully capture what she yearns to say.

"Please, don't cry. Please. Here—here's a Kleenex." Emma pulls a Kleenex from her pocket and offers it to Hannah.

"Would you like to come sit down with me for a minute?" Emma asks. She holds Hannah by the elbow, and Hannah tries to move. One foot, then another, the store a blur. Hannah is shaking as she walks. Her shoulders shake. Yet she walks, slowly, slowly, with her sister (is this a dream, or is this real?) through the rows of red and white. Slowly, she walks around a shelf of maps, and on past rows of little bottles, and a sign saying SUPER VITAMINS! SPECIAL TODAY! High up, over the bottles, a man and a woman wear white coats. Hannah sees them in a blur, and distantly she wonders whether she should fear them. Yet here is Emma, right beside her.

The girl gently guides Hannah to a chair. So much to say! How to start? Close by a man is opening his wallet and giving money to the woman in the white coat. "Pretty brisk out today, isn't it?" he says in a big voice, and laughs.

The girl sits in the chair next to Hannah's.

"So," she says.

"So you escaped?" asks Hannah, in English, and then, in a cascade of words, her questions spill out in her real language. "*From Drancy? Our neighbor, Mme Joupert, wrote to me in—in England. A friend got the letter to me somehow. Mme Joupert said you had—something had happened to you—at Drancy, just before—the trains east. It was in March. So she was wrong! I knew it would be so—I have always known this. I knew the lists could not be right. How did you get out? Who helped you?*"

The girl looks confused and yet kind.

"Could you open your purse for me, so I can help you? If I can look at your wallet, maybe I can find out where you're from, or who to call." The girl points to Hannah's purse, on the silver—

"Tu as besoin d'argent?" asks Hannah. *"Je peux t'aider."* She opens her purse, the silver click-clack thing. She opens her wallet and looks for paper money to give to Emma. Not French money, American. One dollar, two dollars, five dollars, twenty.

"Voilà," she says. It is difficult to come to this country and to have no money. Hannah is lucky to have help, her cousin, in Brooklyn, New York. She sleeps on Julianne's couch, she cares for Julianne's children, and at night she goes to school at the City University while Julianne cares for Mir. Now she can help her sister—she has waited for this all her life!

The girl looks surprised.

"Oh, I don't need your money!" She holds Hannah's hand for a moment, and gently bends Hannah's fingers, so the money curls up inside. "You should put that back in your wallet. I just am wondering if you have some kind of identification."

For a moment Hannah is worried. *Une carte d'identité,* the girl is asking for?

"Oh, I—*mes*—" Hannah is uncertain about her papers. Where are they? And are they in order? Why does Emma need to look at them? Perhaps she has difficulty with her own.

"Who helped you with your papers?" she asks Emma.

"My papers? I . . ."

Of course Emma may not wish to discuss this; it is a field full of mines; one is unsure how to walk through.

"I am your sister," Hannah assures her.

Emma looks frightened. What has frightened her? Hannah looks up the row, and over at the white uniforms. Is someone here? An officer?

"You are safe now," Hannah adds. So much her sister must have gone through! A child of seven, then of eight, of nine. How can a child comprehend such things? You live with your family, in your house, and then you are all taken roughly away, and your mother and father have no power in the face of this. You thought they were big, and you see how they are small.

"Could I? . . ." Emma brings Hannah's wallet out. "I am just hoping maybe you have a phone number here. Oh, look! See? Here's a card, right here."

The girl slips a—paper—out of Hannah's wallet. " 'Hannah Pearl. A resident of Tikkun: Quality Living in a Caring Jewish Environment.' Is this where you live?"

Hannah is doubtful.

"Here's a number to call. Or, what about this one? 'Miranda Luce McCarthy.' She's at a museum in Hartford. Is she someone you know?"

Of course Hannah knows Miranda! She cradled a baby once—Mir.

"Oui, je la connais."

"You know Miranda McCarthy? Should I have the manager call her?"

Hannah looks at the paper in the girl's hands. Should she say yes? What will happen if a manager calls?

"Is she related to you? Is she someone in your family?"

"You are also of my family." Hannah holds Emma's hand. She wishes to hold her hand always.

The girl slips her hand out of Hannah's and rises quickly. "You wait here, OK? I'll be right back." She walks away, down the row of toothbrushes and toothpaste, and then out of sight.

Wait, Hannah wishes to say. But it is Hannah who must wait. Looking at the toothbrushes and the medicines, Hannah feels as if someone has cut flesh from her side. *Mon cœur.* When will the girl come again? How can she vanish like this? She is here, and then she is gone, leaving Hannah to bleed.

A bald man comes up. He wears a white shirt and a red— around his neck. He rubs his head as he sits down in the chair next to her.

"Mrs. Pearl, we've called your friends at Tikkun, and also your daughter, Miranda McCarthy. I'm glad we could reach them. Someone will come as soon as possible from Tikkun." He touches the red—on his neck. "You must have had quite a day!"

"I—" Hannah begins. Quite a day. Yet something remains to be done. What is it? Something must be said—but to whom?

"You just sit here comfortably and someone will be here any minute. I hope they bring a coat for you! It's starting to snow outside."

The bald man stands up. "I'll be right up front. You OK there?"

"My—" Hannah begins.

"Your?"

"*Ma sœur.* My sister. Emma. Is she—?"

113

The man looks puzzled, and then he says, "Oh, you mean Emily? She's up at the cash register. I'm glad she could help you."

The ice shatters. How is it possible to continue to breathe? If you are air, why must you bring air in, let it out? It would be good to have done with this life.

A man walks by, carrying a basket the color of—Hannah is not sure what the color is.

"Afternoon, Fred," says the bald man.

The other man nods and says, "Hello, Sal! How's it going? Think spring's ever going to come?"

An old woman is standing in front of the toothbrushes. She looks first at one brush, then another. All is slow and quiet now, wrapped in gauze, and Hannah too is covered in gauze. She closes her eyes, and then she is in another country. She is about to get onto the ferry for England. The port at Le Havre is crowded and anxious, with so many trying to leave, children on their own and children with families; she is about to say good-bye to *Papa*, who has come with her on the train from home. She has her visas and her passport, her letter from the Cliffords, her letter from the friends who claim her as their cousin. His face is pained, yet he tries to smile. *Au revoir, Hannah. Sois sage, mon cœur. Be wise. All will be well, you'll see. Write to us! And we will write. Write! Write! And Hannah begins to throw her arms about him, frantically, and then the dream skips and she is on the ferry, waving to Papa, and on the deck beside her is Emma, in her blue hat, waving too. So they let you come, after all! she says to Emma, and Emma says* oui, *they said I could come. Han-*

nah puts her arm around her sister's shoulders, and blows a kiss to Papa, who is now a tiny dot on the horizon of France. Over the boat seagulls whirl and cry. May I feed the gulls? asks Emma. Hannah gives her a small roll, and Emma flings bits of the bread out, out, over the gray water.

"Here you are, Hannah!" Hannah opens her eyes to see a woman standing in front of her, in a coat the color of—clouds, ocean, in rain. She is one of the ones in white, at—home. She is the one who frowns, Hannah thinks.

"You had us scared there for a while. Thought you'd have a day on the town, I guess. Here's your coat." She helps Hannah stand up. "You must have frozen your toes off!"

"Emma fed the gulls."

"Did she? That must have been fun."

Hannah starts to walk. She's in a store with all kinds of useful things in it: dozens of soaps, shampoos, lotions, she sees, lined up in cheerful rows.

"Have a good Valentine's Day, Mrs. Pearl!" says a man in a white shirt.

"Oh, she will," says the woman walking with Hannah. "She has a bunch of flowers waiting for her in her room."

Outside the glass doors, white is floating and spinning. All the world is white and gray. Hannah's head is cold; snow swirls onto her face.

"This way, Hannah. Watch your step! How you could have gotten out is beyond me. And they should have told me you had your slippers on. I would have brought your shoes. How in God's name you got out with your slippers on and

115

no coat is a mystery. Someone must have been asleep at the desk, and I hope it wasn't me!"

As Hannah moves, first one foot, then another, she looks into a big window. On it dance hearts, so lovely. Inside, a girl looks over her shoulder. She smiles and waves, yet her eyes look sad. Oh, Hannah knows this girl, or someone just like her!

In the park, a small child in yellow boots is running, running, across the snow, a woman following. Light lingers in the arms of the trees. No police anywhere. A gull flies overhead in the whiteness, crying. It comes to Hannah how the world is cold and beautiful, as she has always known it to be.

SOMEONE NOT
REALLY HER
MOTHER

I am coming with you?"

Miranda McCarthy's mom sits in the front seat of the old white Peugeot, hunched up like a child, her eyes large and frightened. Rolling down the windows to let in the warm air, Mir catches the salty smell of the marshes. She pictures how they spread out, a plate of blue and gold, half a mile away.

"Yes, Mom. I'm taking you shopping for shoes, remember?" Mir hopes she sounds calm; it will make her mom more nervous if she shows her impatience. She adjusts her mom's seatbelt.

Conor will be reading the paper on the side porch now in Wethersfield, in his old T-shirt and jeans, cradling his third cup of strong coffee with O'Hearn at his feet. He likes a slow Saturday morning, no matter how many architectural plans wait for his combing through, or how many chores he has at home. A Saturday is a Saturday, to be embraced slowly and luxuriously. He's always bothered by the way Mir rushes to do this, do that, just as she's bothered by his cheerful refusal to notice what needs to be done—the caulking of the bathroom tiles, the clearing out of the gutters, the hauling out and washing of the screens. I'll get to that this weekend, he always says. But he won't. Weeks will pass, and finally Mir will call some handyman or gardener, at great expense, something Conor will find wholly unnecessary. Of course, he thinks she's right to visit her mom.

"Can I put your purse in the backseat?"

"Ah! Non!" Her mom clutches the purse with her thin fingers.

Her mother's residence sits in the sun, a gray shingled contemporary structure with lots of glass, and ornamental grasses growing along the walk. The large forsythias, in early spring a bright burst of yellow, are an ordinary summer green now. On a long bench, her mom's friends, Helen Goldberg and Rose Sagal, sit smiling and talking. They wave to Mir and her mom, and Mir waves back as she starts the car. Her mom looks up into the branches of the young birch trees to the side of the wide and well-tended front lawn. She often seems to gaze at trees these days, more than at people.

As Mir tosses her own purse into the backseat, she sees an old man walking slowly toward Helen and Rose; he's a newcomer, Helen told Mir this morning, his wife having died recently of cancer in New London. He walks carefully, leaning on a wooden cane, his wisps of hair tossing in the breeze. Howard something. Mir wonders if he has daughters or sons who visit, and grandchildren, as Rose and Helen do. Ruth Zuckerman doesn't; her children live in New Jersey, yet visit only once or twice a year, around a holiday. Ruth often sits in the common area doing a crossword puzzle, or staring out the window—at the birds, she says. She has a heavy accent—German, it sounds like. "Come and sit," she says to Mir's mom. "Come look at the birds with me." All of the other women still have their own apartments in the residence. It's only Mir's mom who now lives in the assisted living section, which is a bit more drab and infirmary like, smelling of lemon Lysol. At least her mom's room is clean, although it's smaller than her apartment had been, and has just one window.

Mir looks in the rearview mirror and over her shoulder, slowly backing up.

"*Je dois venir avec vous?*"

"You don't have to come with me, but I thought you'd like to, Mom. We're just going to the shoe store. I'll have you back at Tikkun by lunch. We'll have lunch together at Tikkun, remember?"

Her mom looks worried. This will be quite a morning, thinks Mir, as she takes a right turn out of the parking lot, and rolls down a block, past old clapboard houses, and a sprinkling of newer ones, expensive by the looks of them. One has a bright yellow door and a tricycle in front. After lunch, she'll visit Fiona and the baby, press her face into the baby's soft neck to breathe in his sweet gingery smell.

"*Je ne sais pas,*" her mom says vaguely. "I should be at home."

Her mom is fidgeting with her purse, opening and closing the clasp, slipping her hand inside for a moment. Mir almost decides to turn the car around and take her back to Tikkun. Why is she doing this, anyway, bringing her out to buy shoes? Mir could just use a catalog. For whose benefit is she pulling her mom out of her familiar room? Her mom doesn't recognize this town; she doesn't enjoy being out in it. Here she is, her hands shaking, fluttering to her cheek, her neck. She has not the least iota of an idea who Mir is. Maybe Mir is a Nazi or somebody, a crazy person, taking her to God knows where, a camp or something. It's so perplexing. All her life, Mir's mom presented a calm face to the world, and barely spoke of what had happened in Europe. A handful of memories slipped out, small ones, of an important day here or there, yet so calm these too sounded. Well, not calm exactly, but shaped, polished, like pebbles at the shore's edge, stories she knew by heart, about someone else, not her. It's just that, even as a child—especially as a child—Mir could feel the presence of grief.

"You like the shoe store, Mom. Remember how you always used to go there, even when you lived in New Haven? It's just a couple of blocks away, on the town green. See? Here's the house you always liked, with the herb garden in front." Mir nods at the old house. In the border, in front of a low stone wall, she glimpses the silvery, upright sprays of lavender, purple at the tips.

Her mom brings a Kleenex out of her purse and bunches it up in her hand. She's mumbling something to herself in French. A few words come clear: *les autres . . . il faut*. What others is she talking about? What necessity?

"And here's the house with the widow's walk." Mir points

up and to the right, at the wedding cake of a house, topped with the glassed-in room. Someone has put a telescope near one of the large windows, facing toward the sky. "I bet you can see all the way to the water from there. At least, you could once, I guess."

Her mom looks doubtfully out the window, not up, but toward the sidewalk. A young woman in flip-flops and khaki shorts is pulling a red wagon holding two small children, heads covered with blue sun hats. (A Winslow Homer, thinks Mir, taking note of the angles of their hats, the color's change, in sun, in shade. The catalog copy for the show is due next week. She'll have to go in to her office all day tomorrow, and Conor will be irritated.). As Mir slows for the stop sign, she sees one of the children start to cry, pointing to the sidewalk; the woman bends to pick up a white toy animal, maybe a seal. Fiona had a seal like that once.

Ahead lies the Congregational Church, large and white, and the green opening out in front of it, with the row of small stores along one side. Mir slowly passes the church and turns left. Placid in the sunlight sit the gift shop, with cut glass in the window, the new French restaurant, St. Anthony's Catholic Church, the bookstore, the chocolate shop, the grocery store, the drugstore, the shoe store, and a handful of others. You would think the whole world was this peaceful, if you didn't open a newspaper. What had Ida just written, though? Someone had set fire to a synagogue in a town in the south of France. Mir tucks this fact into the inner drawer she reserves for all the things she cannot tell her mom. Bullying its way into her mind, the thought she always has—as looming as those rocks Kensett painted from his studio—a question she and her mom always walked delicately around, ignoring: should she have brought Fiona and Ida up to be Jewish, like Mir (although she has little Hebrew, never became a bat mitzvah), or Catholic, like Conor (although of course he's wholly incensed by the Church, but then isn't that what it is to be Catholic?)? Instead, they are "free of religion," as Conor likes to say—ignorant of their heritage, Mir worries. This is one of the questions she has learned not to ask anymore. She is trying to live in the present.

Pulling the Peugeot into a space a short walk from the shoe store, Mir says in what she hopes is a cheerful voice, "Here we are." She turns off the engine and rolls the windows up to an inch from the top.

"Je viens avec vous?"

"Yes. You're coming with me."

Mir wonders if her mom recognizes these stores. Her uncharted outing last February brought her to the drugstore. It was then that Mir had to acknowledge her mom was beginning to—not to vanish, exactly, but to become someone not really her mother. She had not known before how slowly someone could disappear, just a little bit at a time, and then a day comes and you discover that it isn't even as simple as this, that it's you who's vanished from this beloved person's sight, as if the earth opened and swallowed you up. You haven't gone anywhere; you're still right here; it's just that you're invisible. Not even a ghost, for at least ghosts are mourned.

Her mom is sitting in her corner as if Mir is still driving, oblivious to the shoppers walking and bicycling by. Mir puts her blue purse-strap over her shoulder and gets out of the car. She opens the trunk to pull out the walker, which always surprises her with its lightness, and then she opens her mom's door. Slowly, her mom unfolds out of her hunched position. She puts her feet out of the car tentatively, as if to find a dry spot in water, and Mir helps her stand up, all five feet two of her. Is she growing even smaller? Mir notices her thinness, the way she stands only as tall as Mir's shoulder. Her white hair, still pulled back in a bun, is wispier and more flyaway each time Mir sees her.

The curb is hard to negotiate. Mir is upset with herself for having forgotten to park in a spot for the handicapped, if one was even open. She holds on to her mom's soft arm with one hand as she pulls the walker up onto the sidewalk with the other. Stretching to put on the walker's brakes, she feels her mom tipping backward.

"I've got you," she says, as she quickly moves to steady her and help her grip the handles again. Sweat prickles Mir's forehead and upper lip; a flush of heat inundates her. What a hot day it has become.

Slowly, her mom places one old lady's caramel-colored shoe up onto the curb. With an effort, Mir supporting her, she brings up the other and stands shakily on two feet.

"Merci. Vous êtes gentille."

"You're welcome."

Mir is relieved that her mom appears to hold some measure of trust in this woman whisking her into town, saving her

125

from a fall. Her mom takes a couple of small steps and then stops, turning to Mir with a puzzled look.

"Is today my birthday?"

Mir wipes her own forehead with the back of her hand. Her hair is drenched.

"No. Your birthday's in March. You just turned seventy-six in March, remember? This is June."

"*Juin?*"

A look comes into her mom's face, as she pauses on the sidewalk near the drugstore—an inward look—that Mir recognizes as an effort to remember something. She commands herself not to go crazy in her efforts to help her mom remember. After all, her mom spent most of her life—certainly her life in this country—trying to forget. *Who's this, in this picture?* Mir would ask, holding up one photograph or another. Smiling faces, cut sharply in black and white, of lean and handsome figures, often with children, sitting on stone walls in sunshine, or on a pebbly beach, or at cafés (*where?*), would look out from another time, another present. *Oh,* her mom would say, a pained look on her face. *What does it matter now? That world is gone.*

"*Juin, c'est—*" Her mom gazes across the street at the green, as if June could be discovered halfway up one of the soaring beech trees. Mir feels the sun on her neck. If only her mom could keep moving forward. It's unsettling, how often she speaks in French now. Fiona's bothered by it, because she studied only Latin and Spanish in school. Ida's French is getting better and better; she's immersed in the language now. Mir is proud of her for sticking to her job at the *Herald Tri-*

bune, in spite of its frustrations. She's barely made it to copy-editing, and it's writing she's after. And what else is Ida up to? Mir is used to not knowing, yet it's painful. She feels helpless, standing on the other bank of Ida's moat.

"Are you trying to remember something about June, Mom?" Mir touches her shoulder.

"*Oui.*"

"Shall we keep moving? We're almost to the shoe store."

But her mom is looking at the sidewalk, as if she's reading a message invisible to Mir in the gray surface. Mir sighs. So what else is she doing today? Standing here in front of the drugstore, in this heat, she can barely think about her office, the phone calls she has to make.

People come in and out of the drugstore with newspapers and plastic bags, some of them glancing at Mir and her mother and then looking away. A couple of teenaged girls stroll past, wearing bikini tops under loose white shirts and drinking cans of Diet Coke. Mir wishes for a moment that her daughters could be that age again. Ida is the one Mir worries about the most; always it has been this way. For two years now, she's mentioned no boyfriend, yet when she's home someone very polite and probably older calls her at odd hours. *Could I speak with Ida, please?* Afterward, Ida is more quiet and restless than usual; she looks at Mir as if pleading with her to say nothing. Conor says, "She's grown up. You have to let her make her own mistakes." And does life always have to contain such mistakes?

Mir turns to look into the drugstore window, laced with

red-white-and-blue banners in anticipation of the Fourth of July. A bucket and shovel sit in the window, next to a little mound of sand, a big thermos, and a row of suntan lotions. What had her mom been asking about, in this heat? Oh yes— the month.

"June is the beginning of summer," she offers, feeling the sweat trickle down the center of her back. "Ida graduated from college a year ago this month. And it's Fiona's birthday soon; she'll be twenty-six."

Her mom looks blank.

"You used to love June," Mir adds, "because your summer vacation started. You'd sit in the garden reading, all afternoon sometimes, and I'd bring out my paints."

Her mom smiles a little.

"Do you remember reading in the garden?"

"I sat in the white tree."

This is the kind of conversation she always has with her mom now. She thinks she's almost reaching her; she thinks they're in the same place together, walking along arm in arm, almost; and then she comes to a huge lake, an ocean really, and her mom is somewhere on the other side of it, barely visible.

"The white tree?"

Her mom hesitates. Mir can almost hear her trying to think in English.

"Flowers on it."

"Do you mean in Rouen? In your garden in Rouen?"

Her mom looks surprised. "You know this city?" she asks. *"Ce jardin?"*

Quick tears come to Mir's eyes.

"I didn't see the garden with you, but I did see your house, Mom. We visited Rouen together one summer when I was in college, remember? A while ago! We stayed in a little hotel near the cathedral. You showed me your old house. The woman living there had a dog that barked at us, do you remember that?"

Her mom appears to mull this over. Mir can't help her tears. She rummages in her purse for some Kleenex to wipe her eyes, and it comes off looking a dingy salmon color, from her makeup, with wet spots of black mascara. Oh, why does she bother? She looks at her reflection in the drugstore window, to see how much her mascara has run, but her face is barely visible; the sun must be hitting the glass wrong. Oddly, she can see her mom's reflection more clearly, an old woman holding on to her walker, her head bent down as if in prayer.

Mir touches her mom's chin, hoping she'll look at Mir. She does, yet her eyes appear almost glazed over. Mir smiles hesitantly and strokes her soft cheek.

"Let's go, OK? The shoe store is just a couple of shops away."

She nudges the small of her mom's back. A bunch of boys in Little League uniforms walk by, eating potato chips out of a big bag and pushing each other. Mir sighs and looks at her watch: eleven fifteen already. She hopes they won't be late for lunch.

How can this memory of their visit to Rouen have disappeared from her mom's mind? They stood together at the bevelled glass door, waiting, while the little dog flung itself at the glass, showing its pointy teeth as it yapped. When a well-heeled woman finally came to the door, she held it open only a crack, as the dog pawed and tried to get out. Her French was too rapid for Mir, but her mom told her bitterly, as they walked away, that the woman claimed to know nothing of the house before she and her husband had bought it, ten years before, in 1957. It occurs to Mir that if she had not shared this day in Rouen with her mom, it would have no further existence in the world.

"Je viens avec toi?"

Her mom looks confused still, yet a little hopeful now, too. At least she's moved to the familiar form of *you*—a relief in itself. Mir tries to smile, as she holds the walker and moves it forward, one hand on her mom's elbow. They start to walk again, past the drugstore window, and then the bookstore. Books sit on a long table outside; Mir glances at a huge illustrated book on Provence, all yellows and blues and greens. She can't possibly pause to open it; at this rate, she and her mom may never reach the shoe store. It might as well be a continent away.

"Yes, you're coming with me. You came with me when we went to Rouen, and you're coming with me today. Today we're here, in Connecticut, shopping for shoes."

Her mom stops again, and looks at Mir.

"I have shoes at home."

"Yes, I know. But your black ones pinch, remember? And your old comfy ones—these caramel-colored ones you're wearing—see? They're too old; they're run down in the heel. And you keep wearing your slippers instead of real shoes. The nurses are afraid you don't have enough support and you'll fall. I thought we could find you some shoes you'd really like. Remember how you agreed to come look with me?"

Her mom walks carefully.

"*Maman* bought me shoes," she says, "to go away in."

The hot day grows cold. All Mir can think is: here it is again, in this sunlight, on this sidewalk—history. The story unfolding constantly, in circles, the thing you always think you can outrace, only you can't outrace it, because it's here. You're in an ordinary place, just walking along, oblivious, and then you blink, and here again is the day cut out of time—one that glints like a jagged mirror, painful each time you touch one of its poignant edges. New bits, once in a while, bring surprisingly fresh pain.

"She bought you new shoes to go to England in? You never told me that."

Her mom looks up, as if surprised to see Mir.

A woman walks out of the shoe shop carrying a large white bag with the logo *East/West*.

"*Ma mère, vous la connaissez?*"

My mother, you know her?

All right, thinks Mir, here's what I could do: I could just give up. I could sit on the sidewalk and just cry. I could just cry, and my mom could continue to ask her crazy questions, or maybe she could ask other people, whoever walks by— "*You know my mother?*" And she could walk off with some-one much kinder and more patient than I am, someone untroubled by the shadow of a terrifying story always un-folding, and after a long, long time, like next month maybe,

I could stop crying and try to figure out how to live the rest of my life. Because it's not so simple to create a life independent of hers. I think I've done it, and then, in some horrible moment, I picture again the yellow star, the clothes tossed into a suitcase (*vite! vite!*). I am in the train, just as she is, even though she was not in such a train; she was not in such a place; the star was not on her clothing; the banging on the door was not for her, but for the ones she loved. I wake up in sunlight and wash my face, yet my dream is more real than the morning paper on the driveway, more real than O'Hearn sniffing hedges on the morning walk.

How long can a war last? It inhabits you; you are its landscape, whether you suffered it or not, whether you were born before it or after it, whether your parents continued to live, or vanished from the earth somehow (unbearable to think how), to become a face in a photograph, a yearning.

Her mom's face is open and alert for a moment, as she looks questioningly at Mir with her green-gray eyes. Mir urges herself to say something. Yet all she can think is that this woman, Hannah Pearl, née Hannah Luce, was so beautiful once! Her hair auburn and thick, her face quick and lovely. Of course Mir's father, Russell Pearl, must have loved her.

She has a certain beauty still (Mir smiles at her mother), although today her makeup seems to have been daubed on by a child, stopping in a brown line an inch before her right ear, and her white hair looks as if it has been blown on and twisted by imps; her bun is nearly undone. Mir should have helped her fix it more tightly before leaving her room.

So. You can't just sit down and sob. If her mom had done this when her father died—if she had just given up—where would Mir be now? What do her mom's friends do, each morning, noon, and night, with this sweet shell of a woman, holding on to her history even as she has no idea you might be part of it? The thought of Helen and Rose helps, how they take it in stride, just carry on. Any distraction, any errand, no matter how small or ridiculous, can save you.

"Mom, how about coming into the store with me and trying on some shoes?"

Her mom looks disappointed, but to Mir's surprise, she dutifully begins walking again. In a minute Mir pushes open the heavy glass door of the shoe store (*East/West* in silver lettering) to a rush of cool air in a light and airy space. Handsome shoes have been arranged artfully on various levels of genuine-looking maple structures. The saleswoman is one Mir hasn't met before; she's wearing low heels and a short skirt, a blouse of white silk. Mir and her mom are the only customers.

"May I help you?" the saleswoman asks.

"My mother would like to look at some shoes. She needs a couple of pairs, really, one for every day, and one for more special occasions. Both should be flat, though, and give her good support."

While the woman measures her mom's feet, Mir notices that her mom appears agitated. Standing for the measurement, she looks this way and that around the store, as if she sees people that make her nervous. Her hands clutch the walker so tightly that her knuckles look white.

"Mom, are you OK?"

Her mom looks at her, startled, and then her face is irradiated with something Mir can't quite define—gratitude, she'd say, if she had to put a word to it.

Once her mom is sitting again, she half-whispers to Mir in a tumble of French, and Mir quickly translates what she can. Little makes sense, until she realizes that her mom is addressing her as *Maman*. This is a first; she's mistaken Mir for other people once in a while, for over a year now— her cousin Julianne, who died ten years ago, or her neighbor in Rouen, Mir forgets her name—but never her mother. Mir glances nervously at the saleswoman, kneeling next to them, curious and baffled; her French must be worse than Mir's.

"I'm not—" *your mother,* Mir is about to say. Yet the presence of the saleswoman, listening, makes her hesitate. And why must she say this in any case? She wishes she were on the porch with Conor now, being the wife he wishes she could be, sitting still for once, talking companionably, instead of rushing off, cleaning the floor, making phone calls. She dives into bed these days with the covers up, her nose in a book, at eight o'clock at night, too tired to do anything but read. This is how romance ends, with your nose in a book! Or else she could be at Fiona's kitchen table, baby-sitting Seamus, or even in her office, her desk cluttered with paperwork, anywhere but here, in a cheerful shoe store, watching her mother's mind crumble.

"*Pourquoi?*" her mom is saying now. Mir tries to follow, translating the rush of words. "*Why? Why,*" something

something—Mir can't catch it, *"and not come yourselves?
Why did I have to live in—the other place,"* (does she mean
England?), *"sans toi?"* without you? *"sans toute la famille?"*
*without the whole family? "Why could I not stay with you,
as Emma did?"*

"Excuse me," the saleswoman says. "Would you like me
to show you some shoes?"

"Shoes. Yes, I think so. My mother's just a little worried
about something."

"Should I show you some shoes that would be good for
walking?"

"Um, yes, maybe a pair or two. I'm not sure we'll last
much longer here, to tell you the truth."

The woman smiles nervously. "I'll just go have a look,
then."

Mir turns to her mom. She says quietly, "You know your
mother tried to save you. That's why she sent you to England
as an au pair. The Germans were about to invade France! She
didn't know what in God's name would happen. She would
have saved all of you, if she could have."

"Ne m'abandonne pas. Je veux rester avec toi."

Don't abandon me. I wish to stay with you. For one long
moment, Mir is caught up in that day, in early May 1941.
She is her mother's mother, young Mme Luce, of Rouen,
whose family is in the midst of something terrible, the *Boches*
raging toward France, as grimly as in a dream. Refugees are
spilling west, in cars, on bicycles, whole families. It is impossible to know what to do.

"You couldn't stay with her. She was frightened enough,

staying in Rouen when so many people were trying to escape the Germans. She thought you would be safer in England."

Her mom shakes her head vehemently. *"Mais non!"*

Mir gazes at her, not a woman in her seventies now, but a fifteen-year-old girl, rubbing her elbows and trying not to cry as her mother helps her pack her suitcase. On her feet, a pair of new shoes.

"What do you think would have happened to you if you'd stayed in Rouen?" Mir is half-whispering now, looking over her shoulder to make sure the saleswoman hasn't come back into the room. How could her mom not at least be grateful for her own escape? Such gratitude could never be simple; Mir knows this. Of course her mom might always carry with her images, cut in dazzling light, of a house, a room, a mother, a family, a whole world, almost completely vanished now, yet somehow clearer, more real, than what came after. Yet she herself lived.

I would have saved you. Is that what she's saying? *I could have saved you, and all of us would have gotten out.*

"Mom, you can't think that way. It's over and done with. You were fifteen years old, for God's sake."

"Tu ne m'aimes plus?"

You don't love me anymore?

Could this be it? Could it be that her mother's deepest sorrow is about something more even than the invasion by the Germans, or the Occupation, or what came after? That it's about something in addition to the history she had to breathe and move in, day to day, minute to minute—something in addition to her grievous loss? Could it be that, at the core, it's a question of love? Could it be this ordinary a logic, yet this misguided? Emma was kept, proving that Emma was loved. Hannah was sent to England, proving that Hannah was not loved. And of course, if Hannah couldn't save her family, this became further proof that she was unworthy of their love! No matter that Emma died, a child of nine or ten, of pneumonia or something unimaginably worse, at Drancy, in March of 1943. No matter that Hannah's parents died at Auschwitz, or that Hannah had a whole new world ahead of her: a marriage, a child, a life of teaching. No matter. No matter. No matter.

"Of course I love you. I love you very much. I've always loved you." She adds, "And I am very glad you got to England safely, and then here. Very glad."

She holds her mom's hand, and her mom squeezes and holds on tight. If Mir could just dissolve now, into a pool of water on the floor. If she could dissolve, and clean her mind of all this, become water.

"Shall we try these?" The saleswoman walks briskly over, holding two boxes.

Mir glances at her mom, who is sitting quietly now, looking at Mir's hand in her own. If she can just do this, and get her mom back to Tikkun in one piece, maybe she will be all right.

"Mom? Do you want to give these a try?"

The shoes are of a supple leather, a light cream color, much more elegant than her mom's old Naturalizers.

"Will they give her good support?"

"Oh, yes. You wouldn't believe how well these are made. Those Italians really know how to make shoes."

Her mom allows the saleswoman to untie her old shoes, and to slip these on. Even the laces look less geriatric, more fashionable.

Mir helps her mom stand up.

"How do they feel?" Mir says anxiously. What part of her history will her mother start in on now?

To her surprise, her mom looks at the shoes and smiles.

"Very nice," she says simply.

"Try walking," Mir suggests.

Her mom takes a few small steps.

"Je les aime."

"You like them? Good."

Mir squats beside her, pressing down on the toes through the legs of the walker.

"Is that your toe, there?"

"Oui."

Mir looks into her mom's face. "I think that's a good fit. Nothing pinches or hurts?"

"Non. Merci bien, mon cœur."

Mir smiles, surprised. My heart. This is what her mom always called her in the gentlest moments of her childhood. And does it really matter, after all, if she thinks I'm her mother, or her daughter, or some woman in a shoe store? Her mom smiles back.

Mir turns to the saleswoman. "OK, I think we'll take them. Can she walk out in them?"

"Sure," says the saleswoman. "Did you say you wanted others, too? Something more dressy?"

"I think that'll be it for today. I think we're doing fine as is."

"Do you want to take her old shoes with you?"

"You know what? I'd be grateful if you could just toss them."

The saleswoman rings up the purchase as Mir's mom waits patiently, holding on to her walker. As Mir opens the door, the hot, moist breath of summer pulls them outside. Her wedding day, so long ago, in her mom's garden, was just this hot and humid. Fiona's too, in the restaurant near the beach. Ida will come to visit in August's dog days. This afternoon, the baby will be wearing just diapers and a T-shirt, his legs pumping up and down as he squeals at Mir.

"C'est mon anniversaire?" her mom asks.

"No, your birthday's in March. This is June."

"I am in England in June."

"Yes. You were in England in June. But not this June. This June you're staying right here, in Connecticut. Fiona's coming to visit you tomorrow. Remember Fiona and the baby?"

Her mom gazes at a large oak tree on the green.

"I have new shoes."

"Yes. Do you like them?"

"Oui, madame." Her mom looks at Mir, a luminous smile appearing on her face. *"Je t'accompagne?"*

Mir touches her elbow. The heat shimmers all around them.

"Oui, Maman. You're coming with me."

TO AIR,
WORLD, GOD

So much to do! So much—paper—oh! Hannah will save each one; each one will find a place to hide. One must be quiet! Outside her—glass—the leaves, red, gold, shake with happiness. She is encouraged! Courage is within her. She knows just what to do. If only someone does not come in to say, Oh, Hannah, time to clean up for lunch! Oh, Hannah, what are you doing?

She touches the—documents—some the color of clear sky, some yellowed and in bits, some white, and here's a little book in a child's hand, and here's a packet tied with a—something—like what one uses to catch scuttling shell creatures, hiding under rocks. String! She caught them once, with the water crashing against the big rocks; a child caught them once. Here's how you do it, she says, putting squidgy bits on the end of it, putting it into the water. Now wait!

Hannah will not be caught now, if only. She looks at the open door. In the—outside her room, someone is humming;

the one making the beds is humming. She has a big voice, warm. How are you today, Hannah? she shouts in the morning. Hannah does not know if she will come in here. One must be quick!

The box is all in a jumble. Here's a letter, *Dear Grandma, March 21, 2001*. 2001! Could this be right? How fast time is! Hannah reads:

> *Do you remember what I told you, in October, about the person I fell in love with? I hope you haven't mentioned this to anyone! Anyway, I think I know what to do now. I was such an idiot! I think I'll be all right now, being on my own in Paris is heaven.*

What is this about? Something important, Hannah is sure. Much more is here, about walking in the Champ de Mars, walking to work at the *Trib*. The *Trib* is a newspaper, of course it is.

> *I think I'll be able to write some good stuff here. This morning I wrote a draft of a new poem as I sat in the café near my apartment. The people in the café know me now. I love to be known! It makes a foreign country less foreign. Maybe I'll fall in love again! I wish I could see you soon. Love, Ida.*

Who is Ida? Did she not know an Ida once? Hannah calls for her in the darkness. She is beside herself with worry, until the girl comes into the light of the porch. *I wasn't in any danger, Grandma*, she says, *don't cry! See, I'm fine! I just liked it under the tree. I'll come in now, don't worry*. And now, here is this Ida—*being on my own in Paris is heaven*. It is a puzzle.

Hannah folds the paper *(par avion)* once, twice. Bending sideways from her chair, she opens her first drawer, with her lingerie. Mounds of soft clothes, and a small—something—of silk, with a scent of the yellow fruit, like oranges. In goes the letter *(Love, Ida)*, under a bra.

Hannah touches the other leaves—sheets—of paper. Her hands tremble. *Le 14 octobre, 1942—ma chère sœur.* Now this one, Hannah knows. She knows how it goes, without looking, yet she looks. In Hannah's real language, in big letters, carefully written with a nib pen, a couple of blue blots, come words in a child's voice. Hannah translates:

> *I am friends with Julie now. She and I are writing a book together, about an island a long time ago, it's called* L'Ile d'Honneur. *School is all right, but my teacher is not kind! I hate math. I hope the war is over soon. I miss you. How is London? Papa has lost his visiting rights at the hospital, but his patients still come to him. Today Maman has bought six eggs, and even some* chèvre. *Mme Joupert says to say* bonjour. *I am busy now. I have to feed Auguste, remember it was always your job. He's getting very old and fat, and all he does is sleep in the sun. Yesterday would you believe he clawed me! I have a bandage on it, oh well. Au revoir! Je t'embrasse, Emma.*

Hannah pictures a small Emma chasing the cat. Of course Auguste will scratch if you try to stroke his belly. He doesn't like that at all! In the cold room, in the English city,

smelling of wax polish and coal, Hannah cries on her pillow, yearning for Auguste's soft weight on her chest. She
holds him cradled like a baby, and Auguste licks his paws
slowly, first one, then the other, his eyes half open. On a
sunny day, Auguste lies like a round loaf of bread on the
stone wall, under the tree. In the—after the winter—the tree
is covered in white flowers. In summer, the cherries are ripe;
she and Emma must pull out the ladder and pick them for
Maman. Emma cries when her basket spills, and Hannah
scolds her as she helps her pick the—cherries—up. She
makes Emma cry more by her words. How could her sister
be so clumsy?

For days the kitchen is filled with the scent of cherries.

What is this paper Hannah holds in her hand? *Je t'embrasse, Emma*. Evidently, Emma will be here soon. Someone
in one's family, someone one loves, no matter how young and
silly, comes again, Hannah is certain. The baby comes. Others too—the young woman with the name like a flower; the
girl who stands by the window, looking at the floor; the
pretty woman who brings Hannah out, to a restaurant. Is
this real, or is this not real? Hannah holds this letter in her
hand; she walks slowly, slowly, without her—silver thing on
wheels—to the window. Outside the glass, the tree waves, the
leaves tremble and then fly. *That time of year thou mayst in
me behold*. Inside, on the—place by the—window—flowers
arch out, yellow, white.

> *When yellow leaves, or none, or few, do hang
> Upon those boughs*

~

(*Listen to this one,* says a young man, his hair rumpled, as he lies in the yellow light of a bed, a book in his hands. *Oui, j'écoute.* In full summer.)

Hannah slips the letter with the blue blots (*ma chère sœur, je t'embrasse*) inside the flowers. Is the tree bleeding? A tree cannot bleed. Two old women sit together on a bench. For whom do they wait?

In her chair again, Hannah catches her breath. Such a lot to do! She is not used to being so busy here, is she? Outside her door there is just the woman, carrying the coverings for beds. Hannah knows her name, but it does not come to her. The woman does not look into Hannah's room. She is calling to someone, "Good morning, Mrs. Roth, how're you doing today?" It is lovely, such cheerfulness, but Hannah hopes she will not come in.

Now, in her hand, a sheet of paper that opens up. This one has a duck on the front. The duck is slipping on—glass (*non!*). Ice. Its hat flies off. Its—rubber shoes—come off; one is upside-down in the air. Inside, *January 2nd, 2001, Hi Grandma!*

> *Seamus had a blast with you yesterday. He always likes to see you! I hope you got some rest after we left. Today is freezing so I couldn't take Seamus out for a walk, especially 'cause he looks like he's coming down with a cold—such a miserable boy! I want to bring you out here by the water once it's warmer. Hodge is thinking about building a little deck out back. He says he misses his carpentry. When you come, we'll sit under an umbrella and sip lemonade and watch*

*Seamus rip up all the flowers I'm hoping to plant, if
he's crawling by then, oh well. Take care, happy new
year again, love, Fi.*

This one makes Hannah smile. So it's all right, then; the
baby is all right. A cold is no matter. A new year is a happy
thing. Once, a—cold season—comes in, bitter and damp.
Upon those boughs. A room in a foreign country is a cold
place. A baby coughs and coughs, into the night. *Upon those
boughs which shake against the cold.* Hannah puts the kettle
on, for steam. The baby cries. Hannah holds her as she walks
in the little kitchen. Of course a child cries, in such a world.
Against the cold. If the child did not make such soft weight
in Hannah's arms, she could walk all the way from London
across those empty meadows, to a cliff by the English Channel, and hope to perish.

Is she sleeping? Yet, in her hands, a paper with a duck.
And here's another, just a white piece of paper, *le 10 juin,
1943,* it says, and *Hannah Luce,* written neatly at the bottom. Hannah looks at it for a minute—

> *Outside the greengrocer's*
> *window, a Citroën*
> *rolls by, the yellow*
> *of my mother's dishes.*
> *The traffic is noisy.*
> *Shall I ring you up?*
> *the woman asks, her hair*
> *in a net. She puts two oranges*
> *and a pear in the bag*

This one goes on, yet much is crossed out. Hannah can read the next lines, under the scratches:

> *and I am at the table of my mother*
> *once more.*

The poem continues, hobbling along, but Hannah folds the paper before she finishes the poem. It stirs up something inside her. *I am a poet,* she wishes to say, as a girl, in the English city. Yet how can one write poetry if something enormous is missing? She wonders if she knows what it is—something about dishes, something about fruit, a table. Should words be allowed to make one so sad?

"Is that you, Hannah? You're sitting there so quietly, I almost didn't see you!" It's the woman with the voice that's warm like the color yellow, like a pear tart. She's coming in, carrying—sheets. Hannah covers the box with her hands. Could she take it away? Some things are vanished: the little—sharp things—to cut her nails; the slender, silver sharp things for sewing. Books, too! Titles come to her like so many gifts: *The Metamorphoses. Purgatorio. To the Lighthouse. Geography III.* Hannah pictures her full shelves, in the front room of a yellow house.

"Looking at some special stuff today, huh? It looks like you're having yourself a good morning."

Hannah should say something. She knows she should say something, but she can't think what. Sometimes, the words come to her, inside, yet it's hard to bring them out again.

The woman pulls the sheets off the bed. Now in the air

billows a clean white one. It's a parachute, the wing of an immense bird. The cloth billows and floats down. The woman smoothes it out, bending her arms as if she's swimming. One could make a poem of this; how would it begin?

Now the woman flings the—cover, with many colors—into the air. It flies up, and lands on top of the sheets. Now she bends again, tucking in, making straight.

"It's a pretty day out today, not too hot. You going outside today? I think your friends are outside, Helen and Rose."

"Oh, I—" I have too much to do! she could say, but it's best to stay quiet. Can she find her way outside on her own, or is someone always with her, a girl? Hannah likes to be independent.

"Well, you take care now." The woman picks up the white sheets on the floor. At the door she looks at Hannah and waves. And she's gone.

So much paper! What am I to do with it? Hannah touches a packet, tied with ribbon. It is difficult to undo. Hannah's fingers don't work. The ribbon grows tighter. If only—her little sharp things, for cutting. But voilà! One bit of string comes off the packet's edge, and all the rest slips off. The packet comes apart; oh! Documents pour into Hannah's lap, onto the floor, into the box. Someone will surely say, *Hannah, what in heaven's name is this?*

Hannah starts to collect the ones in her lap; one catches her eye. *December 1940.*

My darling Hannah,
  I am about to go up again. At least up there I'll be

doing something, not waiting. If I believed in God I'd
pray to come down in one piece, just so that I could
hold you again.

It's been terrible in London, I know. You must stay
as safe as you can. If the Cliffords do decide to go to
the country for a while, you should go with them, if
possible. I'll be with you in seven weeks, at least for
two days.

All I can do is think of you. The scent of your hair,
of you. I just want to wake up to you in my arms. I'm
picturing how you look right now, as you read this.

Je t'aime. You know that, don't you? You know that.
                                    All my love, Russell

Hannah sees this boy stepping off the train in his uniform.
She smells damp wool and cigarettes as he catches her up in
his arms, breathing *Darling;* the look on his face, in the
evening, at breakfast, of rumpled amusement. When he is
gone, Hannah feels his shape in the air next to her.

A letter, another, and another. All of them on a thin,
crinkly paper, some of them short (*My love, I think of you al-*
ways), some filled with row upon row of small handwriting
in dark blue ink. Hannah looks here and there, opening one,
opening another. Words catch her up.

Two of my oldest friends, Jack Shoreham and
Henry Collingwood, were lost in Normandy last week;
I just got word. They went up to Oxford with me.
Remember I told you about our idea to start our own
publishing house? Henry had just gone back to France
after recovering from a bad injury.

You must stay safe, Hannah.

I'll hold you in my arms   dawn

                in peacetime

Love

*I can't write poems here. You must, if you can,
Hannah. You must hold to your vision of the world;
it's a better one than mine's coming to be. I could
write satire now, if I had half a chance, but I'm not
sure what it would add to the world.*

When we are married

                threshold

  I wish I could erase terrible to watch   city in flames

             my heart, my darling

the stone wall by my family's house, the pasture

If something happens to you

oranges in a bowl your face

               silk stockings

               cigarettes

            I miss you terribly

one day

how many children would you like?

I used to think the words would always be there when I looked for them, but I'm not certain of this anymore.

Hannah is overwhelmed. So much, Russell writes! It will take her hours to understand all he says. Touching these letters is not like touching Russell, in any case. If he came here, she would be comforted. Yet Russell, too, is in great and terrible need of consolation. Once he is home, if peace is ever declared, will she know how to comfort him?

I saw their plane go down, an immense fireball, falling. For a second, I felt confused; had it been my own plane? How was I holding the controls still, and Trevor and the rest were burnt and falling?

I can't believe in God anymore, Hannah. I just can't. Yet the strange thing is, I still believe in the sacred. Someone's life is sacred.

Once peace comes, Russell lies on the sofa in the flat for hours. Hannah is happy when at least he starts to read again. In the cottage in Kent, with the little garden, sometimes Hannah wakes to see him standing by the window at night, looking out into darkness, smoking a cigarette. *Viens!* Come to bed, *mon cœur*, says Hannah, and usually he comes back to her, yet often, even as she kisses him and wraps her body around his, she wonders where he is.

Looking at these papers in her lap, on the floor (*When yellow leaves, or none, or few*), Hannah is filled with sorrow. These letters, these words, bring Russell to her—but is this real, or is this not real? He is not here, in her doorway. Can spirits talk? *Be not afeard; the isle is full of noises.*

Hannah touches her forehead, and the papers pour off her lap. The floor is filled with sheets of paper, like leaves. She tries to bend and catch them, but her hand cannot reach. She must gather them up and put them in the box, before some-one— But now the box slips out of her hands and bounces crazily, scattering *les feuilles* of all sizes and colors along the carpet, along the floor, all the way to the—glass. The leaves, red, gold, outside the glass, shake with laughter; they fly into the air. The lawn is covered with them. Her room is covered. What is she to do?

Hannah tries to reach some—ouch! Someone else will have to do it; the one with the voice of pears will have to help her. Will she say, *Oh, Hannah, what in heaven's name is all this paper doing here?* Will she look at them? Will she say, *Let's put them all away?*

Hannah is so discouraged. Slowly she pulls herself up, and holds on to the—shiny thing—on the side of her bed. She sits slowly on the cover. Her pillow looks soft. Hannah leans on her hand, and—*tiens! Encore du papier!*—in the middle of her bed is a little book, the color of leaves in spring. Inside, the words in the other language, the one she dreams in: *A l'air, au monde, à Dieu. Hannah Luce, 1945.*

How is this here, then? Outside the window, the one in the book, brambles (brambles!) and roses, thistles too—a garden in disrepair. And somewhere close by, a lane and then open fields, and farther still, cliffs; if you look across the water on a day without a cloud, you think you can see your own country in the distance, yet you can't be certain. Inside this house it's so cold, even in summer, for it is summer now, and the country is at peace.

Hannah opens the book to read. The handwriting is blue. This starts in the language of her heart—in French. She translates as she reads, hovering now on the border between one tongue and another.

> *Today I spooned the cream off the top of the milk, and we ate tiny strawberries we'd found at the edge of a meadow about half a mile from here. They reminded me of Maman's garden, how she always had berries of some sort. We spooned a bit of the cream over them and were in heaven. Nausea arrives mostly in the morning. How astonishing to think I may have some little one inside me now! Russell is so happy—I've never seen him so happy, and after such sadness. I am thinking we must face this question of marriage, and soon; I know his mother and father dislike the idea of our marriage. How could Russell marry out of the Church of England, and a Jew no less? Yet they try to be kind. I will go to France soon—in two weeks, I think. I'm frightened of what I'll find out, but there's no other way. I have to know. I'm trying to make myself write to mes grand-mères, my cousins, everyone, for word.*

Hannah contemplates all this: strawberries, a baby, marriage, knowledge. Something more will come, she is certain—what? She thinks of this girl, writing—surely the girl knows little about what happens. So this is a story of one spring and summer in peacetime, on the coast of Kent.

She turns the pages, one and one and one, day to day. And slowly it comes to her, how this is the summer in which her life is changed. First, in French:

I think I felt the baby move this morning, as I lay in bed, very early. I felt something fluttering, like a hummingbird's wing, so quickly! At first I couldn't think this was the baby, but then it happened again, a delicate flutter. I listened to Russell breathing; I could feel his breath on my shoulder. In the midst of my happiness, though, I think of my family, and chastise myself. I don't want to go to France; I don't want to look at any lists. All I want is for my family to be restored to me, for everything to be just the way it was, yet of course nothing can be the way it was.

As she catches a bit, here and there, Hannah is aware how the first language starts to give way to the other. Soon, all is in English.

Coming away from Paris, I looked out the dirty train window and felt sick. I became so sick, I had to ask the woman next to me if she could open the window.

How can I have this new life inside me, and be so stricken with grief? I could be happiest just being out

*of it, the baby too. I can't tell Russell this, but I feel
that he knows it.*

*I can do nothing. Each thing I do is in a blur now, I
am caught up in a darkness I think I will live inside of
for the rest of my life, if I live.*

*I realized something today: I can't speak in French
anymore, or, if I do, the sound of it, the feel of it,
brings back all the darkness. I long to be with my
mother, my father, I long to speak French with them.
If the earth really holds them no longer, if this is really
true—how could this be true?—I cannot speak this
language I shared with them; it's our language, of our
household, our life. All of it's gone now.*

*Russell is very gentle with me these days. I catch
him looking at me. Today I was peeling potatoes for
our soup, and I must have stopped for a while,
because when I looked up, he was leaning on the
counter, gazing at me very gravely. "Be careful with
that knife," he said, and I started to cry.*

Hannah cannot read further. She knows this story now,
how it comes out. It is not a story only, but a life. Don't go!
she wishes to shout to Russell, striding ahead of her in a blue
morning, high above the water, on the cliff. She's happy in
this moment, to be here, with such a man, to be carrying
their child. Soon she will marry him, very soon, at the reg-
istry office. His mother and father have agreed, reluctantly,
to come. Her own she pulls along after her, always, as a moving object pulls shadows, yet today she imagines the shadows
gaining light, reflecting her happiness. Russell is striding

quickly ahead of her, just off the path, his hair tossing in the wind. He looks over his shoulder and waves to her. Then he points—"Look!" Out of breath already, Hannah pauses to look across the meadow at a seagull hovering, weightless, in the air, above the water. As she looks, a huge noise bursts into the day's balmy quiet, like the blowing up of a house. Hannah looks at the meadow. "Russell!" she shouts, "Russell!" She waits for him, but the meadow is a plate under bright blue sky, and the seagull hovers.

As if from a great distance, Hannah hears a knock, and then a voice. The seagull hovers; the meadow is torn. *Land mine,* says the officer later. *It's a terrible shame.*

"Grandma?"

She looks over her shoulder. A young woman is smiling at her in the doorway, waving to her, holding a little boy in a sailor hat. The woman looks at Hannah's floor and her face is surprised.

"Wow! What's all this?"

She sets the child down and bends to the floor, picking up bunches of paper. What a scattering is here! How has her room become so filled with paper? The woman is laughing now, as the child picks up one bit of paper after another. He runs with a funny—like a duck.

"Seamus! You can help me pick the paper up, but you have to be careful! Don't crush them! Here, you." She catches him and holds on to him, opening up his fist and taking the papers. Holding him with one arm, she opens her purse with the other and brings out a little—something.

"Here. Show Grandma your soldier. And be good while I help her for a second." Quickly, the young woman gathers the papers. She bends and rises, bends and rises, and before Hannah can think what to say, the woman's hands are full. Carefully, she lays all the paper in a box.

"Now, where's the lid?" she asks, and looks in Hannah's closet. "Here it is." She pops it onto the box, and puts the box high up on a shelf in Hannah's—the thing with doors. Hannah almost says, *Attends!* yet she is not certain why the woman should wait. What is in this box? Hannah knows this, of course she does! It will come to her in a moment.

The little boy is playing with his soldier near some flowers by the window. He runs to Hannah's bed and the little soldier climbs up, up, until he reaches the top, near Hannah's hand. It is a gray-green soldier, pointing a tiny gun. The child makes the noises of a gun. The soldier falls down, and then is up again, making noises.

"What's this?" asks the young woman, as she sits next to Hannah on the bed. She touches a little book, green and yellow. " '*A l'air, au monde, à Dieu.*' *Dieu* is God, right?"

Hannah nods.

" 'To the Air, the World, God.' Is this a journal?"

"Oh," begins Hannah.

"I'm so glad to see you," says the young woman, and she kisses Hannah right on her forehead. "Guess who I heard from today? Ida! She's crazily in love with someone—has she told you? A Frenchman, of course. She says maybe she'll bring him with her when she comes in August. Oh, Seamus, no!"

159

She jumps off the bed and rushes to the child. The door to Hannah's bathroom is open, and Hannah sees the woman washing the child's hands at the sink.

"Not in the toilet! Oh, God! What am I going to do with you? Such a monster!"

And does it matter if Hannah does not know the words? Does it matter if she is uncertain how this small book came to be here, on this bed, or what is written inside? She has a sense of something vanished, where something was, yet here comes the child into the room, ahead of his mother. He struggles to climb onto Hannah's bed. His mother holds him under the arms and up he comes, smiling, red faced, looking at Hannah, his hair wild and fine. On his sweater, a plump cat with green eyes.

"He has a new word," says the young woman. "Tell Grandma Hannah your new word, Seamus."

The child looks at Hannah, his finger in his mouth. He leans against his mother and crinkles his eyes.

To love that well which thou must leave ere long.

"You remember it! You can whisper it. Here."

She holds him close, and Hannah feels a warm breath near her ear, scented like ginger, like licorice; a hot, sticky hand on her cheek. She hears a sound, a murmur; she cannot be sure what the word is. No matter. *To love that well.* Outside the glass, behind the child's head, the leaves shake with happiness.

~

ACKNOWLEDGMENTS

I quote in this novel from John Donne, Ovid, and Shakespeare, three of the poets my character Hannah carries with her.

I wish to thank the many friends and colleagues who helped me shape my vision of this novel. I am grateful in particular to those who responded to various chapters with such grace and insight, including Sara Blair, G. Wallace Chessman, Rita Elder, Scott Elledge, Jennifer Green-Lewis, Annabelle Howard, Victor Luftig, Jonathan Strong, Vron Ware, Bryan J. Wolf, and Marissa Wolf. Arnold Joseph gave me a better understanding of Hannah's inner life through sharing with me important aspects of his own life, beginning with his childhood escape from Saarbrücken. Jennifer Boittin shored up my knowledge of French with incomparable care and intelligence. I am immensely grateful to my agent Amy Williams for contributing her spirit, boldness, and keen literary sense, and to my editor Trena Keating for welcoming this project from the start and offering courageous and superb guidance along the way. Emily Haynes responded quickly and thoroughly to myriad publishing questions, and Juliette Gillespie did a beautiful job of copyediting.

The composition of the last two-thirds of this novel, in my new home in Palo Alto, has been nourished by the encouragement and inspiring creativity of Stephen Atkinson, Betsy Mize Currie, Kathryn Dunlevie, Monroe Hodder, Jody Maxmin, Bissera Pentcheva, Ursula Schulte, Kathleen Steele, and Lucy Traeger. G. Wallace Chessman, distinguished writer and historian, has cheered me on. Diane Smith and Marsha Wolf continue to show me the rich and consoling possibilities for love and humor in family life, as do my siblings, Alec and Bob Chessman and Anne Smith. My children, Marissa, Micah, and Gabriel, energetic creators, inhabit this story's very texture.

Finally, I am sure I could not have written this book without the generous wisdom and humanity of Roger L. Goettsche and the luminous presence of M. Lucia Kuppens, O.S.B., and the Abbey of Regina Laudis. And I do not know how to thank my husband, Bryan Wolf, for accompanying me in this writing with a vision astonishing in its clarity and resonance.